the ANYBODIES

the ANYBODIES

by N.E. BODE

Illustrated by **PETER FERGUSON**

SCHOLASTIC INC.

New York Toronto London Auckland Sydney
Mexico City New Delhi Hong Kong Buenos Aires

ISBN 0-439-80264-4

Text copyright © 2004 by Julianna Baggott.
Illustrations copyright © 2004 by Peter Ferguson. All rights reserved.
Published by Scholastic Inc., 557 Broadway, New York, NY 10012,
by arrangement with HarperCollins Publishers. SCHOLASTIC and associated
logos are trademarks and/or registered trademarks of Scholastic Inc.

12 11 10 9 8 7 6   8 9 10/0

Printed in the U.S.A.   40

First Scholastic printing, November 2005

Typography by Karin Paprocki

THIS BOOK IS DEDICATED to you. *Yes, you.* Don't be so shocked. Haven't you always secretly thought that you deserved a book dedicated to you and to you only? Well, here it is. Enjoy it. I worked hard, you know, getting all the details just right, just so. Go ahead, start reading. Don't linger here all day. I mean, I know you're pleased and all about the dedication, but you need to get on with it. *Turn the page!*

PART 1
The Swap and the Unswap

PART 2
Things Aren't Always
What They Seem

PART 3
The House of Books

PART 4
The Diary

PART 5
Sweet, Sweet

the ANYBODIES

PART 1

THE SWAP AND
THE UNSWAP

1

A FLUSTERED NURSE

FERN DRUDGER KNEW THAT HER PARENTS, MR. and Mrs. Drudger, were dull.

Ridiculously dull.

Incredibly, tragically dull.

Mr. Drudger enjoyed discussing sod and lawn treatments. Mrs. Drudger collected advertising fliers that came in the mail, bargains on oil changes and mattress clearance sales. They gave Fern birthday gifts like a set of toothpicks or instruction manuals on how to build filing cabinets. They liked only dull things such as toasters (4), sponges (127), and refrigerator magnets (226)—and not those cute bunny shapes and such, but informative freebies from the plumber, the electrician and many from the firm where they worked, Beige & Beige. The Drudgers were both accountants. They didn't like to take vacations from Beige & Beige, but didn't want to cause a stir by not taking them either. So they loaded up the station wagon each summer and went to a place called Lost Lake. There was no lake, only the murky impression of one from years past. In heavy rains, it became muddy enough to attract mosquitos. And here Fern would suffer, listening to her parents take turns reading their manuals while she sipped bland lemonade (not sweet or sour) and swatted her bitten ankles.

Fern was not dull. (Children usually aren't. They can

be a lot of unpleasant things, including nose-picky and stinky, but they are not usually dull. Although there are exceptions—Mr. and Mrs. Drudger, I'm sorry to say, were never interesting. They were the kind of exceptionally boring children who enjoyed putting their toys in rows and keeping their pencils sharp. When feeling wild, they might have hummed, but that was about it.) However, Fern was not only not dull, she was, in fact, quite unusual.

Here are some examples: as a toddler—her earliest memory—Fern had once looked at a picture book about crickets, and every time she opened the book, crickets hopped out. She filled her room with crickets. She thought this would make her mother happy, but when she showed her, the tidy woman had a frozen look of horror. Nothing ever popped out of another one of Fern's picture books.

And when Fern had just learned to read, she caught snow in her mittens and the snow turned into pieces of paper with a word on each piece. She took them to her bedroom and laid them out on her desk, arranging and rearranging them until they made a sentence: *Things aren't always what they seem, are they?*

When Fern woke up in the morning, the pieces of paper were gone. In their place, there was only a row of beaded water drops.

She'd once seen a perfectly good climbing tree that,

THE ANYBODIES

on second glance, was really a very tall nun with thick ankles carrying a big, black, half-dented umbrella. Fern, alone, hid behind a big mail box and watched the nun walk to the curb, glancing up and down the street as if lost. A taxi cab rounded the corner and the nun, who seemed befuddled and a little nervous, turned into a lamppost. It was an ordinary lamppost with a loose dented umbrella kicking around it. Fern said, "Hello? Hello?" like you do when you pick up the phone but nobody's there. "Hello?" Fern waited. Nothing happened. So, she picked up the umbrella, a little dazed, and shuffled quickly to her house.

More recently, during the spring before the summer that I'm getting to—if you're patient!—Fern had arrived early for swimming lessons at the YWCA's indoor swimming pool and had watched her brand-new swim teacher, Mrs. Lilliopole, run after a small bat flitting madly over the bleachers. Mrs. Lilliopole jogged after it, chubby and awkward, wearing a skirted swimsuit, a plastic nose-pinch, and a flowered bathing cap. She waved a net used for cleaning the pool. The bat rose up to the glass skylight and then turned into a marble, dropping to the tiled floor before rolling quickly under the door to the men's locker room.

Now all of these oddities were fine. They were strange, of course, and made Fern feel a little off-kilter, as you can imagine, but none of them scared her until

6

the cloud appeared the day after Fern's eleventh birthday that spring. It was a persistent ominous dark cloud,
about the height of a tall man, that sometimes followed
Fern. The cloud looked like a plume of exhaust, but it
seemed to hover just above the ground, disappearing

around corners when anyone else was around. Once she got close enough to feel its windy presence, and the cloud began to draw her in, pulling on her dress, whipping her hair—like the strong undercurrent of a draft you feel when you stand on the edge of the curb as a fast bus passes by. Fern was certain something terrible would happen if she got any closer. She ran away.

Now, keeping this kind of thing to yourself isn't easy to do. But Fern had to. The Drudgers had made it clear to Fern that any of the unusual things she's seen—crickets popping out of picture books and snow notes—were a result of her "overactive dysfunction," meaning her imagination. *No, Fern, those crickets didn't pop out of the book! We had an infestation! We called an exterminator!* Mrs. Drudger had told her time and again. *And don't start with that business of getting torn-up notes from snow!* Mr. Drudger would add, *No, no, no! We won't hear of such AWFUL fibbing!* In fact, they'd convinced Fern that she'd misremembered everything. No one else had seen the crickets, or the snow notes or the nun, or the awful dark cloud for that matter. So Fern stopped telling the Drudgers and started keeping a diary instead. She wrote about the nun, and about Mrs. Lilliopole chasing the bat with the swimming pool net. She kept notes on things that seemed a bit off to her about people who didn't seem to be who they claimed to be: a robin that watched her intently from a branch outside her bedroom window, the pizza delivery man and the guy who worked the Good Humor truck, even her swimming instructor, Mrs. Lilliopole—after that incident with the bat, the woman had kept trying to get Fern's attention with suspiciously stupid discussions about her scissor kick. It all seemed to be leading somewhere, but she wasn't sure where.

Here's one entry:

I'm keeping the nun's umbrella propped up in my bedroom closet. It's some sort of evidence. Evidence of what, I don't know, but I like it. I'm pretty sure that I'm on the edge of something, something like the whole world turning inside out. I will keep you posted.

But this book doesn't really start with a diary or confused nuns turning themselves into lampposts or bats becoming marbles or evil-seeming, low-flying dark clouds. No, no. That's nowhere to begin. (I'll get to all of that soon enough!) One should begin at the beginning. That's what a writing teacher once told me. Begin at the beginning. And end—yes, that's right—at the end. He was a very good writing instructor, the best in these United States of America, many awards and such. So I'll follow his advice.

When Mr. and Mrs. Drudger were still newly married and young (although I doubt that Mr. and Mrs. Drudger were ever REALLY young—in their hearts. Even in their *baby* pictures, they look like miniature accountants, pale, serious, and joyless), they decided to have a baby. They'd decided it would be a fine idea, a right and worthy idea. Not because they liked children. Neither of them had liked children even when they were children! Mainly they decided to have a child because this is what other people did. And so they did, with passionless accuracy.

This would, in fact, have been fine.

This would have been altogether unremarkable, if not for a flustered nurse: Mary Curtain.

Nurse Curtain was new to the maternity ward of the hospital. The morning of Mrs. Drudger's labor, she had seen a mouse in the nurses' room. Although plump and not usually very agile, Nurse Curtain, as soon as she saw the mouse, had hoisted her rump half onto the counter, half into the sink. She bumped her head on the cabinet, and then the second half of her rump tumbled into the sink with the first half. The mouse scurried on. The nurse began to titter, embarrassed. She uncorked her bottom from the sink and flopped back onto the linoleum.

She said to herself, "Tsk, tsk. You're a woman of science. You should know better." Her white nurse's uniform was damp in the rear now from the sink. A small knot was growing on the back of her head from the bump. She looked down at the long run in her thick white stockings, and she began to cry. She didn't feel much like a nurse, or at least not a very good one. She thought of her mother, who'd encouraged her to stay at home and settle down. "You don't have much going for you, Mary, but you're a good cook," her mother had said. "A man can appreciate a good cook."

Had the elder Mrs. Curtain been more supportive, had she encouraged her daughter's medical dreams, would the rest of this story have happened? Like most things that go a bit awry in the world, we could blame much of the following mayhem on a mother. But, in all fairness, couldn't the janitor have done more to keep mice out of the hospital? Wasn't he feeling especially lazy and porkish that summer, doing almost nothing about the rodent population? And, honestly, as far as my research goes, his mother *had* been encouraging of his desire to sing opera, despite his lack of talent. But maybe she shouldn't have supported him; he sang so badly. So maybe this whole story is partly *his* mother's fault, too. It's impossible to say. In any case, we could go on blaming people and their mothers all day. We can't start second-guessing it all now. It's too complicated, and we have to get back to Fern, as this is about her and not about the janitor's mother.

And so, once upon a time . . . (And I do know that you usually say this in the first line. I have written before, stories and such! Do I have to remind you of the literary genius with whom I've studied? And I know, too, that "once upon a time" is usually reserved for fairy tales, but I like the phrase and you'll just have to

THE ANYBODIES

take my word that this is not a fairy tale—despite the fact that a fairy or two might show up. I can't say that one won't. I refuse to make promises like that! This is a story, not a contract that I've got to sign! But the undeniable truth is that this is a true story! Honest! And my prestigious writing teacher once said that true stories nearly write themselves, so you can pretend I'm not even here writing this, because I may not be!)

AND SO, ONCE UPON A TIME, two women gave birth in the same room. And a flustered nurse with a run in her stocking and a wet bottom and the nagging feeling she wasn't really very good at this nursing business confused the two babies. A boy and a girl, no less.

After the doctor had said, "It's a boy! It's a girl!" Nurse Curtain found herself a little breathless from zipping around the room. She was holding one hefty baby under one arm and another under the other. She cleaned them up and got them dressed and then swapped them—plopping one girl baby belonging to the Bone family into the hospital crib clearly marked DRUDGER and one boy baby Drudger into a hospital crib clearly marked BONE. It was a moment of panic. Regrettable. She had no idea she'd even done it.

The only two who could have recalled for us which baby went to which mother were the mothers themselves. And neither of them would ever know. One was

12

unconscious: Mrs. Drudger had opted for anesthesia.

And the other mother, with large brown eyes, wet as pools, lashes soft as moth wings, began to lose blood. She would lose so much, in fact, that she would die.

2

THE DINNER PARTY

THE DRUDGERS NAMED THEIR DAUGHTER FERN.
Mr. Drudger had been in the waiting room while his wife
was giving birth. He'd had cigars in his pockets, but he'd
felt too awkward handing them out to strangers. He
wasn't the type to clap other men on
the back. He'd spent hours shifting
next to a fern, and that's how his
daughter got her name. It wasn't
even a real fern. It was a fake
fern made in China.

By the time Fern was eleven,
during that summer I'm getting
to right now, she knew this story

well, but every time she asked the Drudgers to go over it, she hoped it would change, somehow magically transform into a better story.

"Are you sure that's the whole story?" Fern asked them again one evening in their pale kitchen with all of its accouterments—neatly stacked sponges, lined-up toasters and magnet-covered refrigerator. Fern knew of a very famous Fern, a girl in a book about a pig, and a spider named Charlotte. She'd lied to friends at school that she was named after the Fern in the book. (Frankly, they hadn't been impressed at all.) Fern now begged the Drudgers, "Is that it? Isn't there something . . . more?"

"No," they assured her. "That's it." Mrs. Drudger was polishing one of the toasters with a yellow sponge. Mr. Drudger was jiggling the coins in his pocket. He knew exactly how many were in each pocket because he was a very good accountant.

They were expecting company to arrive any minute at the front door of their house, number nine Tamed Hedge Road. (Tamed Hedge Road? Yes, that was its name, as if hedges in these parts had once been wild and vicious before brave pioneers like the Drudgers wrastled them into the boxy, subservient hedges they are today.) Fern couldn't smell dinner cooking. Mrs. Drudger made meals so odorless they went undetected. Her dinners were so bland that Fern was the only kid in her school who praised the cafeteria cook, Mrs. Bullfinch, for her seasoning. "What's your secret?" Fern would ask. "What's your secret ingredient?"

"Salt," said Mrs. Bullfinch. "And sometimes more salt."

"Mmmm, I like it," Fern would tell her. "Very clever. You're quite a cook!"

Fern only knew that Mrs. Drudger was cooking something now because the kitchen was a little warmer than usual. Fern, you see, is a very ingenious eleven-year-old girl. She has very keen senses. To put it simply: she's smart.

This was a special meal. It wasn't just any company: the Beiges were coming for dinner. The Beiges were the Drudgers' bosses. Mr. and Mrs. Drudger wanted the Beiges' son, Milton, to meet Fern. They were hoping that Fern and Milton would hit it off, bond, and one day marry.

Mrs. Drudger had told Fern that morning, "One day it won't be just Beige & Beige Accounting. Milton will join the team. Then it will be Beige, Beige & Beige, and maybe you can be Mrs. Milton Beige!" It was shocking really, this language from Fern's mother. First of all, the exclamation mark isn't exaggerated. Mrs. Drudger was actually exclaiming, which was extremely rare. It also showed that Mrs. Drudger had an inch of imagination. She'd been peeking into a possible future. It took Fern by such surprise that she promised to be on her best behavior.

But her promise had grown thin. Fern had already had an odd day. That morning when she picked up the newspaper at the end of the driveway, she saw the dark cloud hiding behind the neighbor's hedge-row. She dodged back inside, her heart beating hard in her chest. Then at lunch a man from the census bureau knocked at the door. While Mrs. Drudger answered a few questions about the family's dates of birth, places of birth, exact times of birth on the front stoop, Fern listened from her bedroom window—always interested in the details of her origins—and, when it was over, she watched the man walk to the sidewalk, where he turned sharply and glared at her. Fern couldn't help staring at the man's left hand, which was gray, see-through, one could say: cloudy. He followed her gaze to his left hand, then shoved it in his pocket and shuffled quickly down the street.

One would think that that would be enough for one day. (In fact, my esteemed writing teacher would have scribbled in the margin, "A bit too much." But if I wrote less, he would make a note like: "A bit too thin." And if I wrote about sad things, he'd jot, "A bit too depressing!" and if I wrote about being happy, he'd return with: "Too breezy!" At some point, you have to give up on trying to please and just tell it like it is. And so . . .) But, in fact, that wasn't all.

There was a bird that liked to watch Fern from a branch outside her window. It was an ordinary robin, nothing special about it except the way it observed her so intently. That afternoon Fern had seen it sitting there, and she'd clapped her hands out the window to see if it would fly off. It did, flapping low over the street. A car was coming, and the bird slapped into the windshield, flipping up over the roof. Fern felt suddenly flooded with guilt for having shooed the bird. She watched with a rising panic. The car went on, and the bird was still alive. Its wing was crumpled, but it quickly hobbled up and danced crookedly before walking on down the sidewalk. This in itself wasn't so strange except at just that moment the neighbor's cat, Jinx, rounded the corner. Fern stuck her head all the way out the window to yell at Jinx, to distract him—even though yelling was strictly barred in the Drudger household. But then the bird shook its head and ballooned into the shape of a large spotted dog. This took all of Fern's breath. The cat darted off and the dog strutted on with only a slight limp, not bothering with the hydrant at the corner as most dogs do. Fern, speechless, watched it go.

Fern told herself that all of this was her imagination.

She tried to believe that the Drudgers were right about her—they were so undeniably sensible. But there were certain things that were hard to deny. For example, Mrs. Lilliopole had seen the small bat turn into a marble, too.

After the marble rolled into the men's locker room, Mrs. Lilliopole, stunned and breathless, turned to Fern. "Did you see that?" she asked.

But by now Fern was used to denying the oddities she saw. "See what?" she asked.

"The bat and the . . . the . . . the marble!" Her voice echoed across the water.

"I don't know what you're talking about, ma'am," Fern said as politely as she could. Adults liked politeness, although they aren't always polite themselves.

"Oh, it was nothing, I guess," Mrs. Lilliopole said, glancing around at the empty ceiling.

Fern tried to believe the sensible Drudgers. She tried. But there was some part of Fern's mind that was glowing, singing, rowdy, brassy as a marching band with characters so big and cartoonish they seemed to be careening down a parade route like giant

20

helium balloons. Her only solace was books, and Fern loved books. She read as many books as she could get her hands on. She had an overused library card, now tattered, and she also bought books at garage sales for ten cents a copy. She used her allowance, even though the Drudgers had made it clear that they expected her to use the money on extra school supplies like paste and pencils. Now she had a little library growing in one corner of her room. One day she wanted books to be stacked all the way up to the ceiling along every wall. This, to her, seemed like a heavenly, comforting notion.

Being a Drudger made Fern feel stifled, clamped down, like a whistling kettle building up steam. (Fern had read about whistling kettles; the Drudgers preferred the mute, nonwhistling kind.) When Fern kept asking about the story of her birth while her mother cooked nondescript food items and her father awaited the arrival of the all-too-important Beige family, it was like letting off just a little bit of steam, just a little.

"Can't you make up a more interesting story about my name?" Fern now asked. "Something about a jungle or something?" This, too, was letting off just a little steam, just a little.

Mr. and Mrs. Drudger glanced at each other. "No," Mrs. Drudger said, her face shining metal in the flat reflection of the toaster. "That would be a lie."

"And we've talked to you about lying," Mr. Drudger added, his doughy skin pinking ever so slightly with frustration.

Mrs. Drudger covered the toaster with a cozy the way some cover birdcages at night. (They didn't have pets, birds or otherwise. The toasters were perhaps the closest the Drudgers would ever come to having pets.) She walked to the oven and opened its squeakless door. A scentless steam rose up. Mrs. Drudger turned, catching Fern in a vacant, wide-eyed gaze, and said sternly, "Now narrow your eyes, please."

Fern often stared at Mr. and Mrs. Drudger with her big eyes. In keeping with the label "overactive dysfunction," Mr. and Mrs. Drudger referred to Fern's eyes as "the unpleasant deformity." They didn't like her eyes. They asked her to narrow them so often that Fern felt like she was constantly pulling down the blinds on her own face. Sometimes when Fern looked at Mrs. Drudger, the woman would fiddle with her blouse to make sure it was buttoned to the top button. She'd say, "Fern, stop looking through me like that!" And there was a pinch to her voice that Fern enjoyed. Sometimes Fern would flare her eyes on purpose to make Mrs. Drudger's voice pinch just so.

But now Fern felt guilty for having brought up her birth, for having asked the Drudgers to invent a better story when she knew they couldn't possibly. She needed to be on her best behavior again. The Beiges were coming and she couldn't afford to go off like a whistling kettle. Fern dutifully squinted.

(Here you should take a sip of water or stretch or look around you to make sure that everything is intact. Hopefully the house isn't on fire or being invaded by a horde of some sort. Sometimes I've gotten caught up in a book, and I would have appreciated a quick reminder from the author concerning the outside world; and I swore that if I ever wrote a book, I would include one. So, here it is. Is everything in order? Okay then. Go on.)

Maybe it goes without saying that the Beiges were on time and that they were, in fact, beige-colored.

Mrs. Drudger said, "Hello, come in. So good to see you."

Mr. Drudger said, "So glad you could make it." He hung up their beige overcoats.

Fern watched the Beiges as they were ushered through the living room by Mr. Drudger. They were short and duck-footed. Milton was a pale sausage of a boy. The skin of his neck chubbed up around the tight buttoning of his collar. He had a runny nose, which he rubbed in a small circle. His nose had developed a small ball on the end of it. Because he rubbed it in a circle like Play-Doh? Fern wasn't sure. His mother had a circular, flat-topped hairdo, much like a beige cake, and his father was imbalanced by a heavy paunch.

Mr. Beige and Milton seemed naturally beige. Their skin, like their pants and blazers, were the exact coloring of Mrs. Drudger's puddings. Mrs. Beige may have once been another color, but she wore beige makeup, so it was impossible to say. (In my tireless research, I did try to get baby pictures of Mrs. Beige, but her mother, who was definitely a pinkish old woman, refused to hand them over. "Go away," she said. "My daughter is beige now. Isn't that enough for you?") Fern was watching the Beige family carefully, but they became so deeply camouflaged they seemed to disappear into the beige furniture and wall-to-wall carpeting, even into the painting that hung in the living room (the only painting in the house, it depicted the Drudgers' beige living room, which only further illustrates the Drudgers' dogged lack of imagination). Like camels against a backdrop of sand, the Beiges melted into the living room (and the painting of the living room) so seamlessly that Fern could only see the motion of their beige shoes.

They walked to the dining room and sat down around the table. Mr. Drudger did, too. The Beiges were here to eat dinner, and the Drudgers prided themselves on the efficiency of their dinner parties. Mrs. Drudger had already whisked herself out of the room and back in, carrying a casserole dish.

Fern took her seat, her eyes tightened to small slits out of politeness. She said, "Hi, I'm Fern."

"Yes, our daughter," said Mrs. Drudger.

"She doesn't look much like either of you," said Mr. Beige.

And here Fern tightened her eyes harder and patted down her hair. Fern's hair was another source of embarrassment for the Drudgers. It stood up curly right on the top of her head. She'd forced it into three barrettes earlier, but it was no use. The hair had broken loose and now puffed like a plume.

When Fern was nervous, she often thought of all the things that she would say if she were the type to say what was on her mind. Fern was now thinking that the Beiges must have been wondering how she got her hair to look like this. The narration in her head went something like: *You might think, Beige family, Does she curl it especially? You might think, Is she really trying to look like an orphan from Oliver Twist who can't afford a comb? You might say to yourselves, Did she wake up this morning and say to herself, "Perfect. I look just like a rooster." You may also want to ask if I've been recently electrocuted. But you're stopping yourselves from saying any of this, because you might think I'm self-conscious about the incident—a fork in the toaster or something. But, no. None of the above. I just look like this. It's completely natural.* Often when Fern went into one of the nervous narrations in her head, there seemed to be a buildup of the unsaid that would create such a pressure inside her that she would find herself blurting one final statement that made no sense to anyone. Sometimes it barely even made sense to herself. In this case Fern busted out with, "I didn't jam a fork into a toaster!"

Mr. and Mrs. Drudger were aghast, of course, horrified by the inappropriate, unrelated statement. Mr. Drudger tried to gloss over it by making a measured comment about sod, and Mrs. Drudger said, "Dinner's ready," but with that pinch in her voice.

Mr. Beige piped up about sod, too, relieved. Mrs. Beige added that there was a sale on lawn equipment. She'd saved the flier. It was in her pocketbook. She went digging for it.

Meanwhile Milton pinched Fern's arm. Rubbing his ball-tipped nose, he said, "My main question is, What's wrong with your eyes? How do you see with them all squished like that?"

Fern sighed. "I'm not sure I can explain."

"Oh," Milton said.

He seemed nice enough, although Fern doubted she could ever marry him.

Mrs. Drudger's meals were all about chewing and swallowing. Nothing more. The food wasn't hot or cold. Just warm. The dining room was quiet, so very quiet that Fern had the peculiar desire to start singing. In fact, she could feel the restlessness of an entire choir harking and heralding in her chest, but she resisted. She pressed it down, kept it to herself. And finally dinner was over.

They were about to clear the dishes when something unexpected happened. Fern could tell it was something important. She could sense it. There was a knock at the door, a loud, nervous, one could say *flustered* knock— as if the knocker wanted to show confidence but didn't really want anyone to be home and so rushed it, hoping to get to shrug, turn, and go.

HOWARD AND THE BONE

MRS. DRUDGER WENT TO ANSWER THE DOOR. "I don't know who it could be," she said. And she was right; she had no idea. The Drudgers had few friends, and the friends who did come by always called ahead so they could each write the appointment on their wall calendars and in their pocket organizers.

It had started to rain. Mrs. Drudger opened the door to a woman in a plastic rain hat, the kind you can fold up to the size of a dime and put back in the small plastic envelope it came in. Fern was out of her seat, peeking from the dining room doorway.

Mr. Drudger said, "Fern, we have company. Please sit down." But, knowing her father wouldn't want to repeat himself for fear of creating a stir, she pretended not to hear him and stayed where she was.

The rain cap had bright red flowers on it, and the woman's face was broad, her cheeks like blooms to match the cap. The woman said, "Sorry to interrupt. I'm not interrupting, am I? I hate to interrupt."

"What is it?" Mrs. Drudger asked. "Are you selling something? Do you have a flier? I'll just take the flier." She always wanted more for her collection.

"No. I'm Mary Curtain. I was a nurse. I was your nurse."

"I'm not sick. I've never needed a nurse."

"I helped deliver your baby," she said.

Fern crept closer. She wanted to ask Mary Curtain questions, a hundred questions. She finally had another source of information, and maybe this woman, brightly flushed and now starting to cry on the wet stoop, would have more to say.

Mary Curtain's cry turned into a blubber. Her cheeks bobbed, blotting out her eyes. Her second chin jiggled then wobbled as she shook her head. "I'm so sorry. So sorry. I quit nursing. I was so terrible at it."

A car door slammed and Mrs. Drudger, startled, snapped her eyes toward a car parked in the street. She hadn't noticed it before. "What's this? Look. You have to go. You *are* interrupting, as a matter of fact. We have guests over. Important guests."

But now there was a man standing in the porch light too and a boy about Fern's age. He was a gangly boy with small eyes and a flat head of hair. On one of his pale knobby knees there was a new scar, healed over, no longer scabby, but a fresh scar nonetheless, still angry. The man had fluffy blond hair, graying at his bushy sideburns. His lashes were blond, too, but full. His face was ruddy. His sleeves were rolled up to his elbows and his forearms were tan. He wore saggy blue jeans, but they were too short, revealing unmatched socks, two different shades of blue.

Mary was hysterical. The man said ever-so-gently, "Mary, come now, Mary. You said you wouldn't cry."

"I know! I know!" she bawled.

The man looked up at Mrs. Drudger. "Sorry, ma'am. Mary was supposed to re-introduce herself and then introduce us."

There was a small breeze and from Fern's spot a few feet away, she could smell the man. He smelled like sweet mint chewing gum and a fruity aftershave. He was wearing a white shirt, thin and wet now from the rain and from putting his arm around Mary, who was soaking. His shirt was see-through and revealed a thick white undershirt.

The gangly boy said, "Let me in. I want to go home."

Mrs. Drudger said, "What? What did you say?" She was staring at the boy, her own eyes wide for once. She recognized something in him. "You want to go home and you want to come in?"

"There's been a mix-up," said the man. "I'm the Bone, ah, well, Mr. Bone. This is Howard. This is your son. And, well, you've got mine. A girl."

Fern rushed forward now and stood just behind Mrs. Drudger's arm, and she saw the man who claimed to be her father. And he saw her. Their eyes locked. Their heads tilted softly.

"Well, now, there she is," he said.

This would probably upset the average kid, but to Fern it seemed to be the beginning of something that

might just make sense. She didn't fit in here with the Drudgers. She never had, and maybe this could explain why. Fern's heart was beating so loudly that the noise filled her ears. She felt an immediate tenderness. Her father? She stared at him. Really? Could it be true?

Though hopeful, Fern was still a little suspicious. She wasn't the only one who made things up. Grown-ups seemed to hate lies, but they told them all the time. They switcherooed things and told half-truths and called them "excuses" and "compliments," and this word "euphemism," she'd recently learned, which means you put a big happy bow on something that's

ugly and pretend it's something else—like each summer when they drove into Lost Lake, there was a big sign that said WELCOME TO YOUR LUXURY VACATION RESORT! (Or as in the introduction of my highly regarded teacher's most recent masterpiece . . . isn't it stretching things just a little bit, just a teeny weeny bit, when he uses words like "genius" and "classic" over and over again, even though he's humbly confessing how difficult and strenuous it is to be a genius who's written so many classics?) Could Fern believe this sopping man in mismatched socks standing at the front door?

"I . . . I . . . I have a dinner party with guests!" Mrs. Drudger said. She called her husband. "Dear! Dear!" She scurried to the kitchen. "The guests will want refills! Drinks!" Mr. Drudger appeared in the hall. The Beiges, all three of them, scurried in after him in a big beige blur. Mr. Drudger looked at Fern, the man, the woman, the gangly boy, all dripping in the open doorway. He said, "Oh, my!"

Mrs. Drudger screamed out from the kitchen, "HE'S OURS! THAT'S WHAT THEY SAY!! NOT FERN!!!" Fern had never heard her like this. The pinch in her voice had risen to a shrill whistle, like that of Fern's swim coach, Mrs. Lilliopole. From the entranceway, Fern could see Mrs. Drudger race around the kitchen. She watched her tear open the refrigerator door looking for drinks and then slam it. The magnets collected there, all two hundred twenty-six, flew off and skittered across the floor.

Mary Curtain and the Bone and Howard inched into the hallway. They stood there awkwardly while Mrs. Drudger scrambled to pick up a handful of the magnets and rearrange them on the fridge. There was an uncomfortable silence. Mary Curtain filled it: "The Bone is such a good father," she said to Fern warmly. "Howard and the Bone have been together for a long time, ever since the Bone got out of jail."

Mrs. Drudger tottered back to the entranceway. "Jail?" she gasped.

The Bone made a correction. "I prefer not to say jail. I prefer to say that I was recharging my batteries. I was taking a rest between opportunities." He tapped his head. "There is no jail that can imprison the creative mind!" He smiled, chewing his gum. Fern agreed with the Bone. Jail, yes, she felt she'd been in jail, too, here at the Drudgers', trying to be Drudger-like, but her creative mind had roamed on freely. Whether he was her father or not, she liked him.

At this, the Beiges got ready to leave.

Mr. Beige said to Mr. Drudger, "What kind of a

place are you running here? I've never seen so much *drama*."

Mr. Drudger blanched and sputtered. "Y-y-you know I don't care for this kind of thing! I don't even go to the theater! You know that!" "Drama," "theater," Fern knew these were bad words, things to disapprove of.

The Beiges shrugged on their overcoats.

Milton asked, "Are you a real live bad guy?" His nose rubbing now seemed like a nervous twitch.

The Bone said, "I prefer to say—" but he didn't have a chance to finish his answer. Milton was swooped out of the house, one parent grabbing either arm. The door was slammed shut.

Now here they were all under one roof: Mary, the Bone, Howard, the Drudgers and Fern—although Fern felt deeply that someone was missing.

Howard asked, "Can I pick up the magnets? I hate to see them all over the floor like that." Actually, Fern loved seeing them all over the floor like that. Mess! It felt good.

The Bone sighed, frustrated, as if Howard had said something that belonged to a long, wearisome battle.

"Yes," Mr. and Mrs. Drudger said to Howard. "Surely. Pick them up! That would be lovely." And they both looked at Howard with such love and affection that Fern thought poor Howard would melt.

THE PHOTOGRAPH

HOWARD AND FERN WERE SENT TO FERN'S BED-
room so the adults could discuss the situation. Fern
glanced over her shoulder as she climbed the stairs: Mary
Curtain was still wearing her brightly flowered rain cap,
still dripping. Wringing her pudgy hands, she looked
anxious, but the Bone was calm. He smiled at Fern and
gave her a wink that seemed to mean everything was
going to be all right. Fern winked back at him. It was a
reflex. She was surprised she'd done it, actually, and
couldn't understand why she had. She'd never winked at
anyone before. She ran up the rest of the stairs.

She didn't know what was going to happen. Was
she not a Drudger after all? She'd never truly felt like

one, not really. She'd always felt more comfortable calling her parents Mr. and Mrs. Drudger, and stumbled over the words "Mom" and "Dad." She'd tried "Mommy," "Ma," "Mammy," "Pop," "Pa," "Pappy," "Daddy." But none had ever felt right in her mouth. Had there really been a mix-up? Would she leave with Mary Curtain and the Bone? Would Howard stay here? Would he take over her room?

Fern had decorated her bedroom herself. She was only allowed to open her door quickly when going in or out so that Mr. and Mrs. Drudger didn't have to be exposed to what was inside. The room was small and felt even smaller because the walls were painted a deep purple, and it was crammed with stuff. Books, mostly. Old second-hand books with that old second-hand-book smell. And keys, for another thing. Fern loved keys—roller skate keys, diary keys, house keys, old car keys, bike lock keys, a skeleton key she'd found on the street. She hung them all from small strings attached to the ceiling.

The room was lit only by a streetlight outside the window. One wall fluttered when the door closed behind Howard. It startled him.

"Butterflies and moths," Fern told him. "I only collect the ones I find already dead and pin them up on the wall."

"Very nice," Howard said a little nervously.

"I'm not allowed to have anything in here that's alive. But I've got lichen growing in my closet. Don't tell."

"I won't."

There was also a dented umbrella in her closet, the black umbrella that had once been carried by a nun who was also a tree and a lamppost, but she didn't mention this.

In addition to the keys hanging from the ceiling, there were flashlights dangling here and there, too. Fern switched on a few. The lights swayed, and so did the room's shadows. Fern sat down cross-legged on the floor. Howard stood for a while and then, cautiously, sat down across from her with his knees pulled up to his chest. Now Fern could see the scar on his knee quite clearly. There were a few jagged streaks and a general redness. She didn't bring it up because she knew how she felt when people pointed out her googly eyes and her unruly hair. Even when they said something nice—"Oh, she's got the most beautiful peepers, and the curliness!"—Fern was sure they'd just caught themselves staring and were trying to cover it up with a compliment.

"So," Howard asked, "who's coming after the Drudgers?"

Fern envisioned a lineup of people. "What do you mean?"

"You know, their enemies. Who's the arch enemy coming after them? Who do I have to look out for?"

"No one. I don't think they have any enemies," Fern said.

"Really?"

"They don't like conflict. They don't like anything that's too much. They don't like too-muchedness."

"Well, then, what do they want? You know, what are they trying to get?" Howard asked.

"I don't think they want too much. Sometimes they get a bonus from Beige & Beige after tax season."

"That isn't much to want."

"They aren't wanters," Fern told him.

"Do you know what I like most?"

"What?"

"This." He held out his arm.

"What? You like your arm?"

"My wristwatch!" he said.

Now she saw it hanging loosely around his skinny wrist.

"The Bone doesn't like time. He says it plays tricks on him. But some plans really rely on good timing. I've taught the Bone that much. He finally got me the watch. I wanted an ironing board and spray starch too, but he said no to that."

"I have three ironing boards and six cans of spray starch and I never wanted any of them!"

"Well, there you have it. That's the whole thing, isn't it?"

"What whole thing?" Fern asked.

"You're the Bone's kid and I'm the Drudgers'."

"Do you really think so?" Fern still wasn't convinced.

"Of course!"

"Here." Howard stood up and pulled a wallet out of his back pocket. It was a plain brown wallet, exactly the same as Mr. Drudger's. He handed Fern a small rectangular piece of paper, a photograph. "See what I mean?"

The photograph was of a woman with long brown hair. She was pregnant, her hands cupped under an enormous belly. Her long arms were skinny. She was smiling with her head tucked to her chest. The most startling thing about the woman, however, was her giant, lamplike eyes. "She looks like me," Fern said, and as she did, she felt a tingle sweep through her body.

"No," Howard told her. "You look like her. That's your mother: Eliza Bone."

"It is?" Fern was incredulous. "You think so?"

"Certainly."

The woman looked beautiful to Fern. Her long arms were supporting her round stomach and the baby inside . . . could it have been Fern? It must have been. She thought back to the words once written on the scraps of paper that had been snow: *Things aren't always what they seem, are they?* She stared into the photograph. This was her mother! Her true mother! She'd found her, and

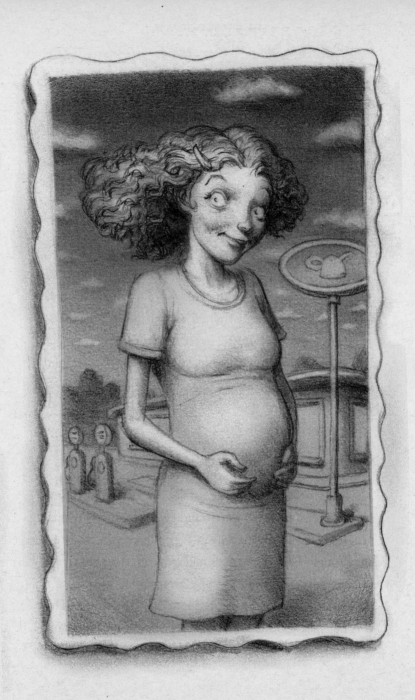

this, maybe, was the thing Fern had written about in her diary, the thing Fern had been waiting for—the world turning inside out. "But where, where . . ."

Howard paused. He pressed his hands together and then he sighed. It was obvious he had something to say but didn't quite know how to put it. "She died," Howard said. "She died giving birth. Don't mention it to the Bone. He doesn't handle talking about it well."

And so it was gone, this hope that had risen up in Fern. It was gone as quickly as it had filled her. She still gripped the photograph, gazing at her mother's soft face.

There was a knock at the door. Mr. Drudger's voice: "Kids? You can come on down now."

"Keep the picture," Howard said. "I'll miss it. I got used to looking at her, but I've got the picture memorized."

Howard started for the door. He put his hand on the knob and then turned back to Fern. He whispered quickly, "Oh, and watch out for the Miser."

"The Miser?"

"Kids!" Mr. Drudger was calling from downstairs now.

Howard nodded. "The Miser."

And they left the room.

THE SCAR 5

"SO, YOU SEE," THE BONE WAS SAYING, "IF WE WANT to avoid any further *drama*, I think this is the best course of action." He was pacing now, hands in his pockets, face stern. His hair was slicked back. Fern wondered when he'd done that. And was he now wearing a tie? How could she have missed a yellow-striped tie? Had he run to the bathroom to put on a tie? Had one just miraculously appeared on his neck? He was talking in a low baritone. Occasionally he would gesture—a firm chop here, a finger point there. Mr. and Mrs. Drudger were enthralled. They sat huddled together on the settee. "Lawyers would only further tangle the arrangement. Mary Curtain is the prime witness." Mary glanced around startled, her mouth a wrinkly O. "You've heard her testimony, seen the documentation"—there was a stack of papers on the coffee table—"and, most importantly, you've seen the evidence." Howard stepped forward, perfectly on cue. "Feel free to look him over."

Mr. and Mrs. Drudger stared at him. They smiled in a buttery kind of way that made Fern roll her eyes. They looked Howard up and down. Then the scar caught their eyes. "What's that?" Mrs. Drudger asked.

"That's the scar that led us to the knowledge that Howard, here, didn't have the blood type of either me or my wife." The Bone's mouth crumpled a little around the word "wife." His eyes glistened. He wiped his nose.

"I told him I didn't want to learn circus tricks," Howard said. "I wanted to go to math camp." Fern groaned inwardly. "I knew I couldn't ride that unicycle. I told you I couldn't."

The Bone explained, "The circus is a fine, long-standing Bone tradition. My mother, God rest her soul, was a trapeze artist." He turned back to Howard. "I thought you were a Bone. I thought you'd take to it like a fish to water. How could I have known you come from . . . from . . ." *Pasty heritage!* Fern wanted to yell out. *From bland descendants! From a long line of dullards!* The Drudgers looked at the Bone, waiting. He cleared his throat and swept his hair back with a soft stroke. "From such perfected stock," he finished, diplomatically.

Mary Curtain spoke up. "Mr. Bone thought that Howard might need a blood transfusion. He didn't. But Mr. Bone is sensitive about people losing blood, because of his . . ."—she paused—"previous loss."

Fern was still holding the picture of her mother. Her eyes filled up with tears, but she didn't want to cry. She wiped them away, hoping no one would notice. But the Bone did. He looked into her eyes. He wilted a little—then snapped to, clapped his hands. "Well, well then. Summer. We'll trade for the summer. See how it goes. No lawyers. This way we can avoid any more . . ."

"Drama," the Drudgers said in unison.

"Good. It's settled," said the Bone.

Mary Curtain lifted herself from the sofa. "I feel that something's been put right. I can't tell you how relieved I am about this. Although I still feel horrible." She busted another gasket and tears spilled down her cheeks. By now, though, everyone had seen enough and ignored her.

Howard was sent to get his bags from the car, and Fern ran to her room to pack enough for the summer. She was nervous, excited. She packed quickly, not bothering to fold anything. She crammed a few of her favorite books in a zippered side compartment of her suitcase and shoved a few new barrettes into her pocket. She took her diary from under her pillow. Fern wouldn't go anywhere without that. She pulled a key with its string from the ceiling, unlocked the diary and slipped the photograph of her mother into its pages. She then snipped the string with a pair of scissors from her desk and turned the key on the string into a necklace. She said to herself, "I'm not a Drudger. I'm a Bone. Magnets and fliers aren't in my blood, neither are lawn treatments or ironing boards. I'm a Bone. My mother had big eyes, and my father's got lumpy hair." She was trying it on, seeing if she could believe it. She almost could. She smiled broadly and then she thought, *My mother is dead*. And the smile slipped from her mouth. She tucked the diary into her bag and, at the last minute, grabbed the slightly crumpled umbrella from her closet, the umbrella that had belonged to the nun, or was it the lamppost?

By the time she ran downstairs, Howard was in the kitchen already eating from a white dinner plate. Mr. Drudger was staring at the boy from across the table. "He's got my skin. He's got my head. He's got your thin neck, dear."

Mrs. Drudger broke away for a moment to hand Fern a few pieces of butterless toast wrapped in a white paper towel and an envelope containing crisp bills perfectly arranged in ascending order. "Good luck, Fern."

Fern felt a nervous speech revving up in her mind, something of the *You might be thinking . . .* variety. But then there was a warm hand on the top of her head, the Bone, and a soft pat on the arm, Mary Curtain.

Suddenly she felt completely calm. "Thanks, Mrs. Drudger. Thanks for everything. And good luck with Howard."

"Howard," Mrs. Drudger said dreamily, "our Howard."

PART 2

THINGS AREN'T ALWAYS
WHAT THEY SEEM

THE ART OF BEING ANYBODY

THE BONE'S CAR WAS OLD, RUSTED OUT. IT growled cancerously. It pitched thick balls of gray smoke out of its tailpipe. The Bone seemed to be volleying more than steering. He'd turn the wheel, and eventually the car would decide to go in that general direction. Every once in a while one of the wipers would bump along the windshield, stall, then bump back again. One of the backseat doors was tied shut with rope that was attached to the driver's headrest. The ceiling lining, which had been originally set at some distant and probably now-abandoned factory, had come unglued and hung like the stretched-out underbelly of an ominous cloud; Fern's mind fluttered momentarily back to the man from the census bureau with the misty gray hand.

Fern was nervous again, and the Bone's driving didn't help any. Mr. and Mrs. Drudger, though not known for their eye-hand coordination, were flawless drivers. They always kept both hands firmly on the wheel, never went over the speed limit or below it. They always used their blinkers. They never cursed and were never cursed at. Fern had been in the car with the Bone for only a few seconds and he'd already had someone blow a horn at him—for good reason, as he'd dipped into another lane for a second—and, though he was clearly in the wrong, he'd blown his horn back. Fern, however, doubted the other car had heard the horn. It sounded like a wounded goose, a very old wounded goose. (I now drive such a car as this, more or less, and I hope one day I can sell this book and become wealthy enough to sell the car, or its handful of working parts, so that I can look back on these days with a deep fondness and nostalgia that can only really take hold when you're poolside, sipping something fruity.)

"You did a good job, Mary," the Bone said. "The tears were very nice. You overdid a bit, just a little."

"I did?" She was rubbing makeup off her cheeks with a hankie, looking into a broken vanity mirror that was attached by duct tape to the car's visor.

Fern was confused. Mary had overdone what? Why was she taking off her makeup?

"Just at the end there. It was too much." The Bone, behind the wheel, shook out his hair so that it fluffed up more on top.

"What was too much?" Fern asked timidly.

"Well, you were very compelling," Mary told 'the Bone, ignoring Fern. "Honestly, I was a little scared of you."

"You were?" The Bone was grinning, full of himself.

"Yes. And where did that tie come from?" Mary asked.

"Oh, it just popped into place. Inspiration, I guess!" the Bone said, clearly impressed with himself.

"What do you mean, inspiration?" Fern asked, a little louder this time.

But again the two up front chattered on. "Well, Howard is always reliable. He's like clockwork. He's dependable. A good kid, in the end." Mary and the Bone seemed very happy, all charged up. They'd succeeded, that was clear. Fern wasn't sure, though, if she wanted them to have succeeded. Were they fakes? Had they succeeded in fooling the Drudgers? Her? Fern's heart started to tighten with fear. No, she told herself, they were nice. Howard, too. Howard wouldn't have fooled her, would he?

Fern sat in the backseat, slumped down low, trying to be invisible. Mary Curtain untied her flowered rain cap and tugged off a wig. And as if her high fluttery voice were attached to the wig, it dropped, too. Mary Curtain was suddenly not Mary Curtain, but a man with close-cropped hair. "It went perfect. I was crying at the end because it was all so perfect. I got emotional."

Fern swiveled around to get a view of her house on Tamed Hedge Road disappearing in the back window. The white house with cream shutters looked like every other house in the row, and now there were more rows of white houses with cream shutters. Fern felt dizzy. She pressed her hand to the window. She thought she might cry. She suddenly missed Mrs. Drudger's blah food, and Mr. Drudger's weedless, blah lawn, which was always mown in perfect lines, which she wasn't ever allowed to walk on. She missed the clean, scentless living room. She was suddenly afraid she'd never see the Drudgers or her house ever again.

Fern didn't start a little narration in her head. No, this time she shouted, "You're liars! Are you stealing me? I'll start screaming! You might think I can't scream, but I can. Very loudly. And you might think that I'm weak, a scrawny little girl, but I know some karate and I know how to bite really hard. You might think that you've got me. But you would be wrong, very, very wrong. I can't tell you how wrong!" And then Fern screamed. She screamed, high-pitched, loud and long. She screamed an enormous, almost perfect, scream.

(Here you could possibly decide that this is an altogether bad book. If these two have abducted Fern in any way, shape or form, then this should be a story with a lesson to girls about always being on guard and never straying from home. If Fern were a boy, this thought probably wouldn't cross your mind. What if Stuart Little had been a girl? We would have arrested her parents for allowing a young girl to set off alone in a motorcar, that's what! What if Harry Potter had been a girl, spirited away by a giant of a man with a magical umbrella? We'd have said, "No, no," and "Tsk, tsk." You may think that girls are better suited to stay in little houses on prairies and within the confines of secret gardens. Or at least working within a buddy system. Wendy couldn't have gone off with Peter alone, you know. Would you have put up with Violet Baudelaire being hunted, on her lonesome, by that man with the singular eyebrow? And there's always that foursome traipsing around in Narnia—Susan, Lucy, Edmund, and Peter—which is fine, because at least they're trying to stick together, protected by their older *brother*. But Fern isn't a boy. She's a girl and she isn't in a buddy system. She's alone. Yes, she's in a car with two men, one of whom was dressed like a woman moments earlier—evidence of trickery. But you'll just have to see it through. And please don't go rooting for a moral about girls being good or punished for adventure . . . like Little Red Riding Hood or Goldilocks. You won't find it here! Not on my watch!)

Finally Fern stopped screaming. The scream had worn itself out, but it had felt very good to Fern, who hadn't screamed for as long as she could remember. Silence filled the car. It was the kind of silence that follows something extraordinary, out of respect, like when you read the last page of great book, and you close it and just sit there for a moment, completely quiet and still. (Not that you'll do that after finishing this book; I wouldn't be so bold as to plant that thought in your mind. No, no, not me!) In any case, it was that kind of silent moment that lingered.

The ex–Mary Curtain was the first to speak. "We aren't stealing you!" he said.

"No, no! We'd never steal anybody!" said the Bone.

"But you're dressed like a woman!" Fern said to the ex–Mary Curtain. "And you, you were pretending! Where did you get that tie all of a sudden and what about your slicked-back hair?"

"We're Anybodies," the ex–Mary Curtain explained calmly.

"Anybodies?" Fern said.

"We're a group," the ex–Mary Curtain said, "of . . . of . . . professionals."

"Professional Anybodies?" Fern asked.

"Exactly!" said the ex–Mary Curtain, as if that explained everything.

The Bone said sharply, "I told you no one knows what Anybodies are." He glanced back at Fern. "You have no idea what he's talking about, do you?"

Fern shook her head.

"Most people don't, you know," the ex–Mary Curtain said to the Bone. "I mean, if everyone knew about us, we wouldn't be doing our job very well."

The Bone said, "Your mother had these gifts as a child." His voice cracked. Fern thought for a moment he might cry, but he cleared his throat and went on. "Some Anybodies are just born Anybodies. Naturals! And some have to learn it, like us. We're practiced Anybodies. Your mother . . ." The Bone paused again. Was he about to cry? He sniffed, rubbed his eyes. "She

was a natural, and when she was young, a book came into her possession, a one-of-a-kind book, and it was called *The Art of Being Anybody*. She was already good, and then she became really, really good. She taught it to me, and I've taught it to a few people, a very few."

"Me, for example," the ex–Mary Curtain said.

"Howard," the Bone said. "I tried to teach Howard."

"And what does an Anybody do?" Fern asked.

"Well, natural Anybodies, who knows? They can do lots of things that I could only imagine. But practiced Anybodies, we can do two things. First: we can be anybody," the Bone said.

The ex–Mary Curtain interrupted. "For example, today I had to be somebody specific. Mary Curtain. And I was."

"You mean you can dress up like anybody else and people will believe you? You mean you're actors?" Fern knew immediately that she'd said something very wrong.

The ex–Mary Curtain erupted, "What? Actors! Please!"

"Actors! HA!" said the Bone. "Can an actor shrink fifteen inches to be a child? The greatest Anybodies of all time could take on the body of a table, of a flea! It's mysterious. It's elevated. It's grand!"

"Oh," Fern said. She was thinking of the bird that she'd seen get hit by the car and how it shivered into a dog. She wondered if a great Anybody could do that. Could a great Anybody turn into a nun and then a lamppost? Could a great Anybody go from being a bat to a marble or take the shape of a mean, gusty cloud? She decided not to bring up all of that. She decided to keep her questions simple. "What's the second thing?"

"Well, the second thing was my specialty," said the Bone. "I could help other people become better versions of themselves."

"But how?"

"Hypnosis and a deep concentration and something else."

"What else?"

"We're not sure. It's a third ingredient. I used to have it, but now I don't. So things go a bit off. I've got some kinks in the system nowadays. And I'm nothing compared with the greatest, most famous Anybody alive today." The Bone lowered his voice to a respectful hushed whisper. "The Great Realdo! I've met him, two times."

"And there is the other master, too, don't forget," the ex–Mary Curtain said. "The Miser!"

There was a hot moment of silence. Fern remembered the warning Howard had given her: *Watch out for the Miser*. The Bone slumped down behind the wheel. He said, "There's no need to talk about him."

"But he has gotten better and better. And we certainly

haven't, that's for sure." The ex–Mary Curtain turned to Fern, confessing, "I was never very talented. Not bad, but never great. Your father was very, very good."

"The Miser is no Realdo and he never will be!" The Bone seemed winded, almost breathless now. It was clear he didn't like to talk about the Miser. He said to Fern, "Look, I mean, the truth is: I am your father. That's the bad news, the sad truth, Fern. I'm a has-been, a washed-up hypnotist, a washed-up Anybody."

"Oh," Fern said. She didn't really understand what an Anybody was, but she knew that being a has-been must be terrible. The Bone seemed to sag under the weight of these failures now. Fern felt sorry for him. It was true that she couldn't really trust a word the Bone said, but still she wanted to comfort him. That was how she felt. She wanted to tell him that everything was going to be just fine and to maybe pat his head or even hug him. But she hadn't ever been in this position before. The Drudgers had never needed comforting. They were so self-sufficient, like wind-up toys that could wind themselves and goose-foot on forever. So Fern, not knowing what to do, didn't do anything about wanting to comfort the Bone.

"You're not so bad nowadays," the ex–Mary Curtain said, but it sounded weak.

The Bone looked at him sharply, then said to Fern, "I'm not a very good father. I won't go around being mushy with you. I don't believe in all that. I get along in the world just fine without it."

"That's okay," Fern said. The Drudgers weren't mushy types. Although Fern was relieved that she hadn't patted the Bone on the head, she was a little disappointed that there would be no mushiness allowed here either—even though it seemed the Bone was often on the edge of tears, which she decided was best to ignore.

"I'm Marty," said the ex–Mary Curtain, reaching over the seat to offer his hand to Fern, who shook it. "I've been friends with the Bone for a long time. My wife and I took care of little Howard until the Bone got out of jail."

"Oh." Fern thought she should say thank you, because Marty and his wife would have taken care of her if the babies hadn't gotten swapped. But it didn't really make sense to thank him for taking care of her, since he hadn't. So she asked a question: "Where is Mary Curtain?"

"She lives next door to her mother right here in town. She gave up nursing. That part was definitely true! It helps to sprinkle in the truth," Marty told her. "It helps give a more convincing performance. Mary Curtain got married. We talked to her and her husband. We had dinner together. She's a great cook. But she's an anxious woman. She would've never been able to go through with something like this."

The Bone was quiet, letting Marty chatter. He kept his eyes on the road.

There was a lull in the conversation. Fern was thinking, trying to process everything she'd learned. The Bone piped up. "I just knew you were my daughter. I knew when I saw you." His voice was soft for a moment, but he didn't let it stay that way. "Well, it was clear as a bell."

"But how long have you been planning this? You didn't lay eyes on me until tonight!"

"Not true. Not true," said the Bone. "Marty delivered a pizza to your house two weeks ago. And I'm the Good Humor Man you've seen. I hate that tinkling music. 'Home, Home on the Range'—a million times a day."

So that's why they had seemed a bit off. Fern didn't tell them that she'd been suspicious. They both seemed to have fragile egos about their Anybody abilities. But it seemed like those oddities in her life, those inexplicable happenings, might just have been real. "And Howard? What has Howard been?"

"I'm teaching Howard how to hypnotize other people, but he isn't old enough to do the transformations himself. Howard kept it running. He kept us on track. He had graphs and charts," the Bone explained.

Fern was putting things together. "Which one of you was the man from the census bureau?"

"What?" the Bone asked. "What bureau?"

"Who?" asked Marty.

"Nothing," Fern said. No, the man from the census bureau had been a bad force. She thought of the Miser and felt that old dread again. But just then something else crossed her mind. They were at a red light in the middle of town. Fern quickly took off her seat belt (the only thing that seemed to work in the car) and looked at the Bone's face. His eyes looked familiar. His chin seemed to jut out just so. Fern stared at him, and he stared back like he was going to ask her a question . . . a question about . . . *her scissor kick*? Yes, her scissor kick! Fern gasped sharply, a yelp really, and flopped back in her seat. "Mrs. Lilliopole! My swim teacher!"

"In the flesh!" said the Bone proudly. "I would have preferred being a softball coach, but you were bent on swimming and there was an opening for a girls' swim coach at the YWCA. And the woman hiring was a real feminist, wanted to hire a woman. That was clear."

"If you cut a Nerf football in half," Marty explained, "and stuff each end into a swimsuit, it gives a pretty realistic look." As a visual aid, he pulled two halves of a Nerf football out of his blouse the way Fern's science teacher used the plastic model human being with removable innards. "Back in our prime, of course, neither of us would have had to rely on such things."

Fern couldn't shake the image of the census bureau

man and the dark cloud. She had to ask: "Could you ever turn yourself into, say, just for example, a bird, and then if a cat came along could you turn yourself into a dog or into—I don't know—a cloud?"

"Us?" the Bone asked. "Are you kidding? Maybe, just maybe, if our lives depended on it, we could have some great sparkling moment. But, knowing us, I doubt it even then."

"You and me? Ha!" Marty said, shaking his head, almost laughing. "Nope. Once the Bone almost became a dog. He shrank to four short legs, grew fur even, but he couldn't get the tail or the muzzle. And it took three days to get even that far. Oh, well. Important thing is that we got him back. It took all of our concentration, mine and your mother's. He could have stayed that way, you know. Odder things have happened."

"They have?" Fern had trouble believing that there were odder things than turning yourself into a dog and getting stuck that way.

"The Great Realdo could turn into a dog in three seconds," the Bone said. "But you know what I mean, Fern. You've seen it happen, right? Remember the swimming pool?"

Fern didn't respond. She wasn't ready to admit to anything, not yet. You see, she was very well trained by now not to mention such things. She sat there, clamped down, eyes narrowed, as Drudger-like as possible. Something loose in the car rattled, a few things actually. Fern held onto the door handle to see if the rattle would stop. One rattle did, but others jangled on.

"I have to say, Fern," the Bone continued, "it was at the pool that things became clear. The bat? Remember?"

Fern stayed perfectly still.

"It wasn't planned. I don't know why it was there. But it was remarkable."

It was *remarkable!* Fern was thinking. She squirmed in her seat. She thought of the whistling kettle. Finally she blurted, "I saw it too. How it changed into a marble and rolled away!"

"I know you saw it," the Bone said calmly.

"You do?"

"Yep. You denied it. That's what made it clear to me that you're mine. Any other kid would have been shocked, would have had a million questions about how a bat could become a marble. Any other kid wouldn't have been able to shrug and go on with their lesson as if nothing had happened, as if that kind of thing—"

"Happens all the time," Fern finished. "Well, not all the time, but often enough. And why is that?"

"You're being watched over," the Bone said. "I don't know why." He didn't dwell on it. But Fern wondered if it was the good kind of being watched over or the bad. "We had to figure a way to get you out. At least for a summer! I'm hoping you've got your mother's

67

head on your shoulders, just like you have her eyes." The Bone said it, but then he blushed. "I don't mean anything by that! The eyes are nice enough. I didn't say they were beautiful or anything."

But for the first time, Fern thought that someone actually meant that her eyes *were* beautiful. She felt shy all of a sudden. She sat back and buckled her seat belt again. She fiddled with the key that hung from the string around her neck. Fern wondered if the circus was in her blood, if she could be an Anybody, if she could turn other people into better versions of themselves. Could she turn the Drudgers into being something other than dull? She wanted to ask questions about the Miser, but didn't. There was one thing that needed to be very clear. Fern didn't want to ask, but she had to. "My mother is really dead?"

There was a pause. "Yes," the Bone said.

Fern closed her eyes. Howard had been right. He hadn't fooled her. She missed her mother now, deeply, and it was strange because she'd never known her, had never known that she existed until just that evening. The missing was more painful than anything Fern had felt before. The image of her mother in the photograph holding her belly appeared in Fern's mind. It was all she had of her. "And the book?" Fern asked. "Her book, *The Art of Being Anybody*? Where is it now?"

Marty humphed and shook his head. "Funny thing," he said. "No one knows. It was in their house before the Bone went to jail. But things were packed up after, well, after, you know . . . The bank came in and took everything out to sell. It could be anywhere, really, anywhere. Not that it would be of much use. It was written in a certain code only your mother could decipher." The car got really quiet then. Even the windshield wiper froze as if holding its breath.

"Or you," the Bone said.

"What?" Fern said.

Marty went on, "Now that we know about you, well, the idea is that maybe you'll be able to decode it. Your mother figured it out when she was your age, and then she could write that way. She even wrote coded grocery lists, sometimes out of habit." He sighed. "The book has more secrets. Many, many more."

"And we don't want the Miser to get his hands on it," the Bone said.

"You needed me so you came and got me! That's the only reason! Because you think I'll be able to decode some book, some lost book!" Fern was angry now, more confused than ever.

"No, Fern," the Bone said. "I came and got you because you're my daughter and, for better or for worse, you should know me."

The rain was letting up. Fern could have told them

that she did have some powers. Hadn't she once gotten a book to cough up bunches and bunches of crickets? That wasn't exactly being an Anybody, but it was something, wasn't it? Hadn't she once turned snow into scraps of paper that asked her: *Things aren't always what they seem, are they?* Yes, she had, and it was true. Anyway, maybe it was nice to be needed, Fern thought, although she wasn't sure she could help at all. She gazed out the front windshield and noticed there was no rearview mirror. "Isn't it dangerous to drive without a rearview mirror?" she asked.

"I prefer to look into the future! I prefer to see what's coming. Why look back, Fern? In life, I mean. It's a waste of time. I never look back. Do I, Marty?"

Marty stared at the Bone but didn't answer.

The Bone squinted out onto the dark road. He seemed distant suddenly. He said, "I can still smell her lilac perfume. Your mother always smelled of the sweetest lilacs."

THE BAD HYPNOTIST

THE BONE STOPPED IN FRONT OF A TRAILER IN Twin Oaks Park to drop Marty off. Marty's wife was hunkered in the small metal doorway. She was a tall woman, so tall she had to stick her neck out, ducking her head down to fit in the small frame of the door. She was wearing a yellow bathrobe, tied too tightly at her middle, and pink spongy hair curlers. Her chin was set in a menacing scowl.

"By the way," Marty said to the Bone. "You owe me money."

"We weren't talking about money, were we?"

"No."

"Then how can it be 'by the way'? It can't be, can

it?" the Bone asked.

"I think it's an expression to say 'by the way,'" Marty explained, a little defensive. "People say it all the time, even when something isn't 'by the way.'"

"Yes, but it should be reserved for when something is 'by the way.' Don't you think?" the Bone said, heatedly. "I mean, what would happen if there was no clear communication? We may as well all speak gibberish. Do you want us all to speak gibberish?"

Marty had to admit that no, he didn't want everyone speaking gibberish. And so, Fern noticed with a bit of pride, the whole issue of the Bone owing Marty money disappeared.

Marty looked at his wife. He mumbled, "Wish me luck," and then he hopped out of the car. The Nerf football halves under one arm, he spread the other wide open and called to his wife. "What are you doing awake? You need your beauty sleep." She didn't move; her glare only tightened on him. "Not that you *need* your beauty sleep. I mean, you're always beautiful . . ."

"What's amatter with you?" Marty's wife started in. "I don't like that Bone character. I told you a hunnerd times. . . ."

The Bone hit the gas to drown her out. The car hesitated, coughed, then chugged off. Fern looked out of the back window. The trailer was lost in a cloud of exhaust. But as the exhaust thinned, the cloud took

on a smaller, tighter shape. In fact, the dark cloud followed, rolling alongside the car like a dirty tumble-
weed. Fern refused to look at it. She tried to listen to
the Bone, who was talking about his house. "Now, my
place, the place I'm living in now, it's just a temporary
dwelling. It isn't fancy. I don't go in for fancy. I like a
roof over my head and plain living." Fern rubbed her
eyes and looked out the window again. The dark cloud
was still there, though it was tripping along, sagging in
on itself with exhaustion. "It's not like Tamed Hedge
Road. It's not a house on a street like that. But it's nice
enough." She rubbed her eyes and looked again. The
dark cloud was finally gone. "And the neighbors are
good folks. You'll see. You'll be charmed. It's quite
charming in a rustic kind of way."

Fern knew what the word "rustic" meant. Reading
books will give you an excellent vocabulary. (My old
writing teacher used to say that reading *his* books and
his books *alone* would give you an even better vocabulary. Although I respect his paunchy belly and his horn-
rimmed spectacles and his way of pronouncing things
much like an overeducated British butler, I didn't
always agree with him on every point. In fact, perhaps
I wasn't his favorite student.) Fern thought she was
going to a farm, a charming, rustic farm. But "rustic"
is a tricky word. They'd driven away from Tamed
Hedge Road, away from Twin Oaks toward seedier and

seedier parts of town. There were neon signs in store-front windows, car dealerships, run-down houses and abandoned lots. The Bone pulled in front of a string of houses separated by alleys as narrow as a rat's rump. He bumped up over the curb, then the car plopped down with a disgusted sigh. The houses backed up to a railroad track. The yards were nearly bald. The grass patches, interrupted by mud-pocks, were mowed raggedly. He looked at his own yard and sighed deeply. A man was standing there, shuffling his feet around, his head bobbing back and forth.

Now, Fern liked adventure. One of her favorite books was about a boy who came home from school to find a tollbooth in his bedroom, and he drove a toy car through it into a different world, which sounds a little absurd to me. But as much as Fern liked reading about adventure, she was feeling a little nervous about the one she was actually having as she stared at the Bone's neighborhood. It was growing dark. There was only one streetlight working. The others looked like they'd been smashed by rocks. She kept an eye out for the dark cloud. Was it hovering behind the tire swing? Was it behind the Dumpster? Fern thought of the Drudgers at their house, where maybe they were teaching Howard to brush his teeth in small circular motions, and she was glad she wasn't there, but was she glad she was here instead?

The Bone got out of the car. Fern did too. She grabbed the black umbrella and her bag, feeling the top for the hard outline of her diary, which held her mother's picture. She slammed the heavy door behind her.

The next-door neighbor, a woman with a mop of blond and black hair, sat on her front stoop smoking. She said, "He been here a good couple hours, just strutting around like that." Aside from the pecking movements of his head and the occasional flap of his arms, the man looked normal, wearing corduroys, a white shirt, an ugly necktie, and a leather belt. He seemed absorbed in the pecking and strutting and hadn't noticed Fern or the Bone yet.

The Bone nodded. He took Fern's bag for her, hoisting it to his shoulder. "We'll have to make a run for it." He paused, then called out to the neighbor lady, "We expecting a train soon?"

"We're always expecting a train soon. They come every five minutes! Only way I tell time. Look, you gonna do anything about him?" the woman asked.

The Bone didn't answer. He lifted his head, straining forward. Fern could hear a small rumble in the distance. "Train," the Bone said. "Wait, wait . . ." The train was getting closer now, closer, the noise rising up. This startled the man. He began bobbing frantically. "Now!" the Bone shouted. The train rattled loudly, creating a gust of wind. The man was squawking. The Bone ducked his head and ran quickly past the man. Fern followed. The Bone was at the door now, rummaging for keys. Fern glanced over her shoulder at the neighbor woman and the man in the yard. The train had passed and the man was settling down.

"I know you know him," the woman shouted.

"I don't," the Bone shouted back.

"He ain't going to howl, is he? He ain't going to start to hoot or something and go all night? I'll call the police if that kind of mess starts up again. You hear me?"

"It'll be fine," the Bone assured her. "He's a stranger. Maybe he's lost. I'm sure he'll go away on his own. It'll be fine!"

But it didn't seem that way to Fern. The man had fixed his eyes on Fern and the Bone. He was now high-stepping it toward them. Just before he was in striking distance—and it did look like he was angry about something—the Bone found the key, jiggled the lock, opened the door, hustled Fern inside and slammed it.

"Who's that?" Fern asked, shaken.

"Who?" the Bone asked.

"That man in the yard?"

"Him? Oh, well. I'm not perfect," the Bone said. "Hypnosis is a tricky business. Anyone will tell you that. Sometimes things go a little haywire. He signed a contract, though. Fair and square. He's got no grounds to come after me."

"You said you didn't know him," Fern said with a
small accusation in her tone. The Bone lied. That's
what Fern was figuring out. He lied a little bit quite
often, and although this made her a little bit mad, she
also understood it. Being Fern Drudger had entailed a

good bit of lying, too. Only now she knew she hadn't been making up the things she saw. She hadn't been fibbing when the Drudgers accused her of it, no. But she *had* been lying in a way every time she narrowed her eyes for them, every time she kept her mouth shut when she wanted to let a choir out of her chest. She'd lied by being the way they wanted her to be. And why had she lied to them? Well, to please them, to make things easier for them. And wasn't that what the Bone was trying to do? He wanted things to go smoothly, for the man in the yard to be a stranger so that everything could be nice, for himself, but maybe for Fern, too. Maybe he wanted Fern to like him.

But here's a little fact: Lying to a fellow liar is quite tough. Liars are the best at catching liars. And so his lies didn't work on Fern. She'd catch him every time. And maybe this was the biggest relief of all: Her lies wouldn't work on him either. She couldn't pretend to be a Drudger in front of the Bone. He'd see right through her, just like he had at the swimming pool when he was Mrs. Lilliopole, wearing the plastic nose-pinch and the flowered bathing cap and the skirted swimsuit. He knew that she had seen the bat and the marble, and she wasn't just any kid, but *his* kid.

"I don't, technically, know any roosters. And that's what he is." Fern looked at him in such a way that he knew she knew better, and he smiled a small, guilty smile accompanied by a small, guilty shrug.

The Bone flipped on the light switch, illuminating a small hallway. There were two doors: one to the right, the other straight ahead. The Bone unlocked the door to the right. "We only have the bottom floor. The Bartons live upstairs. They're clog dancers, I'm sorry to report." (I'd like to add here that the Bartons, though you'll never meet them in this book, are actually quite famous clog dancers—that is, in clog-dancing circles, which tend to be very, very small circles.)

They stepped into the apartment. It was still dark and muffled, too, with a distant *ching*, *ching*, *ching* of little tiny bells. Although Fern didn't know the names for everything she smelled, here were a few: garlic, heavy Indian incense, blooming narcissus, Chinese food gone bad, cedar chips, mothballs, a mix of oranges and onions, and mint.

The Bone flipped a wall switch. A dim light flickered on and at the same time music came on, too, from a radio in the corner—horns and a singer singing, "Hope the sun gonna shine, hope the sun, hope the sun, hope the sun gonna shine on down." The walls were draped in velvety cloths, like in a movie theater. And there was artwork on top of the draping: framed shoe inserts, a fish made out of tea bags, a painting of dental floss, which made Fern think how funny and beautiful and sad life was all at the same time. They were nothing like the single painting in the Drudgers' living room of the Drudgers' living room, which only made one think of the Drudgers' living room. There was a card table with pop-out legs and two folding chairs, an orange knit sofa and a bunch of beanbag chairs that'd seen fluffier days. The Bone walked quickly to the windows that were covered by heavy curtains. He pulled each one back, peering out. "Spies," he told Fern. "The Miser knows something's going on. He's hired a ring of spies. They press their cups against the windows and try to hear what my next step will be."

It was hard to believe that anyone would spy on a place this strange and small and unofficial looking. Fern had a more glamorous impression of spies—for example, that they had equipment that was higher tech than cups pressed to windows—but she could tell that the Bone believed in the spies, even if she didn't (not yet, at least).

Fern turned around in a slow circle, taking the place in. She'd always wanted to feel at home someplace in the world, but was this it? She doubted it. It didn't feel like home, not really, but she kind of liked it all the same. It was so different. That's what she liked about it most of all.

The Bone walked into the cramped kitchen. He could only open the refrigerator door six inches before it hit the opposite wall. "Are you hungry? Thirsty?"

"Both," Fern said.

"I've got an onion. Oranges. A can of mushroom soup." He pulled out some Chinese leftovers, sniffed and tossed them in a plastic garbage can.

"Sounds fine."

"I used to have a dog," the Bone said. "But when we went to the circus, you know, where Howard tried the unicycle, the dog decided to stay. He had some high-quality tricks and, I suppose, thought he was wasting his talent on such a small audience as Howard and me and sometimes Marty."

Fern wandered around the living room. There was still a good bit of dog fur, an extra coat on the sofas.

"Why do they call you the Bone?" she asked.

"I'm as tough as a bone. I'm not at all soft," said the Bone, but he was a little flustered, like he didn't care for the question, like he was lying. "I've always been called the Bone and so that's that."

"Okay," Fern said. She didn't want to upset him.

When the Bone came in with the food, Fern was holding a framed photograph. It was a picture of the Bone and an enormous man with a boxy nose, arched black eyebrows, dark-circled eyes. The two were standing, laughing, pointing at each other.

"Your mother," the Bone said, a hitch in his voice, "took that picture. That guy was my best friend. But not now."

Fern stared at the man's face. She felt a chill. He scared her. She remembered the angry glare of the man from the census bureau and his dark, ghostly hand. "The Miser."

"That's right," the Bone said.

Fern stared into the Miser's eyes. They were the same as the census bureau man's, weren't they? Had the Miser been the gusty dark cloud that had tried to pull her in, closer, whipping at her clothes? Was the Miser capable of turning himself from a bird to a dog with one shiver? But the bird couldn't have been him. She'd liked the bird. It had watched her kindly with its little head cocked and its eyes wet.

"You were once friends?" she asked.

"Yes. Best friends. I keep the picture as a reminder. We grew up in the circus together. The spies are a troop of little people. The Miser knew them from his ties to the circus and hired them away. My mother was a trapeze artist, as I said, and his father was the strong man. He ate nails. The Miser was once the sweet, sensitive type. He was named the Miser as a joke, because it was the opposite of who he really was. He'd write you an apology if he thought he hurt your feelings. We resorted to trickery, but I tell you, he made sure we were always the good guys."

"But now he's after you?" Fern asked.

"He was in love with your mother, see? And she

loved me. He never got over that, I tell you. He got me put in jail as soon as I married your mother!" The Bone shook his head, sighed. "I don't want the Miser to get his hands on that book. It's powerful, and he shouldn't have it! You see, the book doesn't really mean much to either me or the Miser. It's just a big coded mess to the two of us. Only your mother could make sense of it. And he was hoping that Howard would be born with some of Eliza's powers and that he'd understand the book. I guess I was hoping too. It was clear that Howard wouldn't be able to make any more sense of it than we could—he lacks the gifts. But then the Miser found out that you existed, and now he wants that book again because you're the key to unlocking it.

"Honestly, Fern, and I'm not used to being honest, but I want the book because your mother loved it. I can picture her now walking down the street toward me, lost in thought, the book held tight to her chest. That big old leather book with a small leather belt wrapped around it. Your mother kept it safe, always safe." He seemed to drift off a moment here, lost in the memory, and Fern lost herself, too. She liked this glimpse of her mother, a young woman carrying a giant book. Fern could relate to it. She loved books too, and she loved imagining that she and her mother had this in common. The Bone came to and went on. "Now we're both looking for the book. And he wants to make sure he gets it first. Your mother would want me to have it, Fern. Me. The Miser thinks the book should be his, but he's wrong! Your mother left it for me."

Fern wanted to see this book with her own eyes. She wanted to feel the weight of it and carry it locked to her chest. "And you don't know where it is?"

"Nope." He shoved his hands into his pockets. "The book is for me, for you, for us, Fern. We have to find it first. The book holds more secrets. Dark secrets. He could learn how to hypnotize nations, Fern, and he wouldn't do any good with that. None." Fern felt that sense of dread again, the windy pull of the dark cloud. The Bone looked at Fern. She knew her eyes were wide with fear. She hadn't known that there was so much at stake.

"I didn't mean to scare you!" he said.

"I'm not scared," Fern said, but she was lying. It was too late. She was already scared.

The Bone held out his hand and Fern handed him the picture. He sighed deeply. "Your mother, she was the real thing. Before I met her, I could make people waddle around onstage or sing silly songs for the audience. But your mother taught me how to be an Anybody. I was already an okay hypnotist. But together the two of us, your mother and me, we could cure people. Together we never turned anybody into a rooster. We were healers, really. Now I try to cure folks, and that's what happens." He pointed to the front yard, to the rooster man. The Bone turned back to Fern. "Go ahead and eat."

Fern wasn't sure if her hands were shaking because she was frightened or starving, or both. Mr. and Mrs. Drudger preferred oranges so dry and pruned that their white casings were brittle. Their soups were homemade and tasted like wet air. She'd never eaten an onion before, much less a raw one. Here, the orange was so juicy it dripped down to her elbows. The soup, from a can, was salty. The onion tasted like a sharp sting. She gulped whole milk, chocolate, in fact.

The Bone was up and down. He watched her eat some, gazed at the photo from time to time; but he was often drawn to the front kitchen window, where he kept an eye on the man in his yard.

"Is he still there?" Fern asked a few times, anxiously.

"Yep. Still there."

Fern looked around the apartment. There was one neat corner with a shelf of oversized books. Fern could read the titles of the books from where she sat, things like *The Complete Book of Mathematics*. Fern assumed it was Howard's territory. That was one thing she missed here at the Bone's, her small but growing library. All of the books seemed to be Howard's. Didn't the Bone have a few of his own favorites? Fern couldn't imagine going without books. Howard's area was small and tidy. There was a box of earplugs and an air spray, regular scent. Howard! Would he really love being with the Drudgers? Could he? Hadn't he liked something about living with the Bone after all these years? Wouldn't he miss it? Fern already felt different, and she'd only known the Bone a few hours.

When Fern finished eating, she wiped her mouth on her sleeve. It was a test. Mr. and Mrs. Drudger would have scolded her. She wanted to see what the Bone would do. He said, "You like my cooking? I once had an Anybody gig as a French chef. Those were the days!"

Fern imagined the Bone in a puffed white hat. It made her smile. She almost said, "I'm glad I'm here." But she didn't. She was pretty sure the Bone didn't want to hear anything that might come off as soft. He'd told her that he didn't like anything mushy. Plus, she was still getting used to it all. She still felt off-kilter. She said, "I'm glad I'm not still at my house." That was the truth. She was happy to be relieved of math camp and Lost Lake and boredom. But she was scared, too. She wanted to help get the book before the Miser did, but what if she wasn't able to? She was just a kid, after all, and not even the type to be the first one picked for kick-ball, or the second or the third. "What should we do about the Miser?" she asked. "How can I help?"

"Well," said the Bone, "there's a more pressing issue." He looked at a clock on the wall. The clock looked unreliable, at best. It had faded numbers, and the nine had slipped down so that the clock had two sixes. The second hand was inching uphill. It got stuck, then sprang five seconds forward. "Mr. Harton."

"Who?"

"The rooster's name is Mr. Harton. Or it was Mr. Harton before he gave up selling vacuum cleaners door-to-door to become a rooster. And, come morning, he's going to start to crow. But I've got a hunch, I've got a feeling, that you'll be able to cure him."

"Do you think so?"

"I tried to wink at you while I was Mrs. Lilliopole. I was always trying to get you to look at me, but you never would. But then finally I did wink at you, Fern. Remember? When you were going upstairs at the Drudgers? And you winked back. Probably didn't think you were going to wink, but you did. And if an Anybody winks at another Anybody, even an Anybody who isn't really an Anybody yet, they've got to wink back. It's one of the rules from the book. And you winked, Fern. Naturally. You winked!"

3

DEHYPNOTIZING MR. HARTON

OH, MY OLD WRITING TEACHER, SOMETIMES I still think of him, like now, right here at Part 2, Chapter Three, "Dehypnotizing Mr. Harton." If he could see me now, typing feverishly, he would have to admit that I do look like a writer and act like one. I may even smell like a writer, but I'm not sure what writers smell like—ink, erasers, books? He would be astonished, I tell you, because he never had faith in me. Not one ounce! Some teachers just don't know the gem sitting right in front of them. Like you, for example, you're obviously a gem and you probably have one old stinker of a teacher who doesn't have any idea. Well, you'll show that teacher one day, you will, you will!

Like I am at this very moment in Part 2, Chapter Three. Oh, and after this there's more, more, more! In fact, I will promise right here, right now, some very freakish, bizarre behavior and outlandish surprises. Read on!

Before inviting Mr. Harton in, the Bone vacuumed. Mr. Harton had left his demonstration kit behind, and the Bone wanted to use the sample vacuum before he'd have to give it back. He didn't own a vacuum cleaner, and maybe you recall that the Bone's apartment was still very furry from the dog that'd left him for the wider, more appreciative audiences of circus life. Fern watched the Bone's harried vacuuming job. He started out on the orange sofa—Fern had never seen anyone vacuum furniture before. A flurry of motion, he was nothing like Mrs. Drudger, who vacuumed in diagonal rows. The Bone vacuumed the same way he must have mowed the front yard, in ragged, starlike clusters. He'd probably borrowed the mower, too, Fern thought (and she was right). He shouted the story of Mr. Harton over the small, thrumming vacuum motor, and Fern listened intently, trying to dodge the vacuum's zipping nose.

"MR. HARTON WAS A TERRIBLE SALESMAN, FERN. HE COULDN'T SELL FAT MICE TO CATS. HE SLOUCHED. HE WAS SHIFTY-EYED. HE MUMBLED HIS DELIVERY. HE LACKED CONFIDENCE, MOST OF ALL. WITH CONFIDENCE, YOU CAN SELL ANYTHING. REMEMBER THAT,

FERN. THAT'S IMPORTANT. I LET HIM IN BECAUSE HE WAS SO PATHETIC. I TOLD HIM THAT I COULD HELP HIM WITH HIS PITCH. I COULD GET HIM THE COCKINESS HE NEEDED TO BE TOP-NOTCH. SO I HYPNOTIZED HIM. HE LEFT HERE SO FULL OF HIMSELF HE DIDN'T WANT TO SELL VACUUM CLEANERS ANYMORE. HE SAID HE WAS GOING TO SELL CONDOS OR SOMETHING. HE HAD A BROTHER WHO'D MADE A FORTUNE IN CONDOS. SO HE LEFT."

"BUT HE'S BACK. WHAT HAPPENED?"

The Bone had strayed too far from the outlet. The plug popped from the wall. The vacuum cleaner's motor, wheezy from the intake of so much fur, wound down, its stiff lung deflated. "It's the same thing that always goes wrong these days. I'm not exactly sure how it happens. But they seem to . . . they seem so overcome with their new personalities that they turn into some animal version of the trait I've given them. Once a stupid man turned into an owl. And a woman who wanted to have children turned into a rabbit. It doesn't always make perfect sense. Once an old man wanted to be young and he turned into a baby kangaroo." This made Fern nervous. She didn't want to be turned into something ridiculous, and she hoped that the Bone couldn't do it accidentally. She worried about him now, the way you'd worry about someone

91

wandering around with a lit match who could bump into the curtains, setting the whole place on fire. "No one ever showed up at the front door to complain when your mother and I were together. No one ever showed up trying to catch flies with their tongue." The Bone scratched his chin with his knuckles. "The process has developed some kinks."

Fern fiddled with the key on her necklace. She thought of her diary with her mother's photograph in it. She was still not used to the idea that she had another mother, much less one she would never get to see. "Do they have to live like that for the rest of their lives?"

"Oh, no, it wears off in a couple of months or so."

"Months!"

"But you'll be able to set Mr. Harton straight right away. I know it."

Fern was doubtful. "I will? But I have no idea what to do." She wanted to explain to the Bone that she wasn't very good at doing things in general. Maybe there had been some kind of mistake. I mean, so much of what the Bone had said fit in with the strange aspects of Fern's life, explaining some of the unexplainable, but this? Fern was sure she was going to disappoint the Bone, and she didn't want to. He had his hopes pinned on her.

"Don't worry. I'll walk you through it. It helps that you have the gift handed down to you. I don't want you to be just a sideshow act. I want you to be someone who really can help people one day. But there's that other ingredient. The one I had once but don't now." He gazed off for a moment, his eyes catching on the photograph his wife had taken of him and the Miser laughing.

In the Bone's defense (and I do defend the Bone, because although he's kind of a squirrelly guy and imperfect, he is good, deep down), hypnosis is an imprecise science. Actually, when you think of chemistry with its H this and its O that, and when you think of biology with its test tubes and beakers and its dissected worms, well, hypnosis isn't a science at all. And it isn't really an art, either, in light of the Mona Lisa and ice sculpting and baton twirling. And it isn't a sport, because you don't get points or win those statues of miniature golfers or divers glued to marble. So I'm not sure what to call it, but really it's murky territory. It's mysterious, yes, that's it. It's a mystery.

The Bone set to work. He opened the apartment door and then the main door to the house. He walked out into the yard behind Mr. Harton and flushed him inside by clapping and waving his arms. Mr. Harton was all high-step and flap. He stood in the middle of the room, his head bobbing now and then. He stared at Fern and then started to preen. He used his nose like a beak, picking at his shoulders. The Bone rolled the vacuum cleaner over to Mr. Harton, but Mr. Harton didn't even look at it. The Bone rolled it back and forth right in front of him, but again Mr. Harton ignored it.

"That's a bad sign," said the Bone. "He's in deep."

With a little force, the Bone sat Mr. Harton down in a chair next to Fern at the table where she'd eaten. Her orange peel sat in the empty soup bowl with the tough heart of the onion and its crisp brown skin.

"Okay," said the Bone, "try to get him to look at you. Try to catch and hold his stare."

Fern stared at Mr. Harton. He had pale blue eyes that looked a little teary. They darted around the room, falling occasionally on Fern's eyes, but not staying put. Fern moved her face to block his view. She was certain that she wouldn't be able to do it. She was bound to let the Bone down, and what then? Well, terrible things could happen. Mainly, the world could come to an end. But, Fern reminded herself, she wasn't a Drudger who fibbed because of an overactive dysfunction. Her real mother never would have called her a fibber. Her real mother would have understood. Fern caught Mr. Harton's eyes, then lost them, then caught them again. Fern had to try to do this. She had to. She kept at it and, eventually, he was staring at her out of one eye, his head turned away, as if he were a bird with an eye on the side of his head. Yes, she had him!

The Bone slipped Fern a pocket watch on a gold

chain. The pocket watch didn't work, of course. The Bone didn't keep track of time, as you all know by now. But the watch was shiny and, on its long chain, it swung nicely, which were the qualities the Bone looked for in a pocket watch.

"Hold it up by the chain. Make it sway back and forth and back and forth. That's right. You've got it."

Fern was making the watch sway like a clock's ticktock, and Mr. Harton's watery eyes were hooked

on it. Fern was very proud. She smiled at the Bone, but he shook his head. "Not done yet," he said. "More to it than that. Now don't look at the watch yourself, Fern. Don't look at it." He began to whisper into Mr. Harton's ear, "You are getting sleepy. Very sleepy." He kept on with this until the man's eyes blinked again and again, more slowly, until they shut and didn't open.

Fern let the watch drop to her lap.

The Bone handed her a bell, small and brass with a black wooden handle. Then he put his hands on Mr. Harton's shoulders. He said to Fern, "Say these words: 'You are not a rooster. You are a man. Return. Return. Return.' And ring this bell softly, softly each time you start to say it again. Try that."

Fern rang it once, then started to say the words. "You are not a rooster. You are a man. . . ." And the Bone started to hum, a deep low note. Fern felt something electric, a snappy static all around them. Each time the Bone took a breath to hum again it was like a car trying to start up. There was a *vroom vroom* of energy, something buzzing and zapping. But the engine never really revved up. She could feel the electricity rev and stall, rev and stall. But she kept on repeating it, "Return, return, return." She was holding the bell in front of Mr. Harton's face, ringing it softly. Her arms were tired. The Bone's hum was breaking up.

Finally he said, "Okay, ring it loud now. Ring it like crazy."

She did, and Mr. Harton startled awake with a gasp, like someone who'd been trapped underwater coming up for air.

"Stand up," the Bone told him. He did, shakily. He glanced at the vacuum, and it was clear that he recognized it.

"Good. Good," the Bone urged. "Walk to it."

Mr. Harton looked at Fern and the Bone. He looked longingly at the vacuum cleaner.

"What is it?" the Bone asked. "Do you want to tell us something?"

Mr. Harton nodded and then smiled broadly. He pitched back his head and let out a loud clear yodel, a clear timeless cry of "Cockadoodledoo!" Then he put his head to his chest. His face crumpled. His eyes spilled two tears. Fern knew there had been something, some kind of magic charge, and although it wasn't enough, she knew she'd felt it and it was undeniable. She wondered if spies were listening to all of this, if the Miser would hear about this sad failure.

The Bone sighed, and Mr. Harton half-heartedly stepped to the vacuum cleaner, grabbed its handle, and rolled it toward the door. The Bone opened the first door for him, then the second. Mr. Harton, still a rooster man, bobbed his head, but Fern couldn't tell if it was an acknowledgment or simply a roosterlike flinch. Fern and the Bone followed him outside and watched him strut down the street with his vacuum cleaner bumping and rolling behind him.

4

SPIES

THAT NIGHT, THE BONE THREW SHEETS ON A ROW of saggy beanbag chairs—a bed for himself—and sheets on the orange, now less furry, sofa for Fern. They lay down across the room from each other in the dark. Except for the occasional roar of a passing train, the apartment was quiet. There was a little slice of moonlight coming in through a crack in the curtains. Fern was writing in her diary as silently as she could. She had a lot to catch up on. She wrote about Milton Beige, Howard, the Bone, and Mary Curtain—the real Mary Curtain in her kitchen somewhere—and Marty, the fake Mary Curtain. She wrote about the rooster man and the raw onion and the orange and the Miser and her mother, most of all her mother. She pulled the picture out, gazed at it, and then wrote:

When I look at the picture of her, I mean really look, really stare right into her eyes, I feel like I know her. Sometimes I feel like we are thinking the same thing or feeling the same thing, like our hearts miss each other.

The Bone started to hum a sad love song, and then he sang a few of the words, "Sweet, sweet, my sweet darling angel, where have you gone, where have you gone?"

The song made Fern want to cry. She put the picture back into the diary and closed it. She stared up at the ceiling, and a lump rose in her throat. When she coughed, hoping to clear it, the Bone stopped singing. He coughed too, as if embarrassed he'd been caught. Fern thought that maybe he'd thought she was asleep.

"Soon the Bartons will start clog dancing upstairs," the Bone said.

"At least the rooster won't wake us up," Fern said.

"True."

The Bone let out an exhausted sigh. He said, "Your mother knew she wasn't going to make it. She just knew. She told me over the jail phone, looking at me through the Plexiglas. I told her she was silly. She started giving me information about the book, where she'd leave it for me, a special spot, but I hushed her up. I said I didn't want to hear about it. She gave up talking about it. She gave up pretty easily, in fact. She didn't want to upset me. Or, sometimes I think, maybe . . ."

"What?" Fern asked, propping herself up on her elbows.

"Maybe she was hatching a bigger plan. Your mother was tricky. She always had a way of getting what she wanted."

"What did she want when she was alive?" Fern asked, now sitting up and staring at the Bone through the weak light.

"Oh, I don't know."

"Really," Fern said, "tell me."

The Bone thought out loud, "What did she want? What did she really want? She wanted for me and the Miser to be friends again. And I guess she'd have loved it if I'd gotten along with her mother. . . ."

Fern hadn't thought about this before. She had a grandmother. This took her by surprise. She wanted to meet her grandmother now. She had to!

The Bone went on, "But her mother is a loon, I tell you. C-R-A-Z-Y. She runs a boarding house but truly lives in a world of books. And I mean that very seriously. I never got along with the old woman. . . ."

Fern stopped listening now. She was starting to under-stand something—her mother was a plotter. She had a plan. She was smart. She wanted the Bone and the Miser to be friends again. Fern guessed that her mother felt responsible for the two cutting ties, for coming between them, maybe. And she wanted the Bone to become close to her mother. Well, of course, she loved these two people.

Now that Fern knew what her mother wanted, she had to think of how her mother would use the book to get it. Her mother knew the future—that she was going to die—but how far into the future could she see? Did her mother know that one day Fern would be here trying to piece it all together? Fern was on her feet now, pacing. It helped her think.

"What is it?" the Bone asked.

Fern didn't answer because she hadn't really heard him. She was thinking of her mother's heart and her own, her mother's mind and her own. How would Fern's mother use the book to bring all of these people together—the Miser, the Bone, Fern's grandmother, and maybe even Fern herself? Wasn't she part of the puzzle? Did this plan of her mother's rely on Fern? Fern paced some more. One thought turned to the next and the next and finally she knew where the book would turn up. There was only one logical spot. The one place that Fern was most drawn to, the one place where they would all wind up. "Well, that's it then," Fern said.

"That's what?" the Bone asked.

"The book is at her mother's house!" Fern said loudly.

"What? You're joking."

"No." And now she jogged over to the windows and yelled it. "The book is at Eliza's mother's house!" She yelled it again, just because she liked being allowed to yell. "THE BOOK IS AT ELIZA'S MOTHER'S HOUSE!!"

She pulled the curtain back quickly and there, on the other side of the window, was a tiny pale face with a sharp nose. It was a small, little, tiny man with a cup held to the window, pressed to his ear. The ear was big compared to the man's small head. Too big. He stared at Fern for a split second and then took off, running down the train tracks to a red van with gold lettering, too far away to read, a few other small men straggling after him.

"Spies!" Fern said. "And they heard it all!" She was triumphant.

She let the curtain drop and turned to the Bone, who was now standing up, his spine straight, his expression electrified. "Why did you let them hear it? Why didn't you scare them off first?"

"Simple," Fern said. "How could you become friends with the Miser again if he doesn't know the book is at her mother's? And how could you become close to my grandmother if the book isn't there? And how would I eventually know my grandmother at all if it isn't there? We've all got to be there together."

You see, Fern is quite smart. She isn't good at math camp, but she's bright, quick-witted. She'd never known that she was right before. She'd never had that strong conviction. But now she did, and she felt something else that was new: stubbornness. Now that Fern knew she was right, there was no changing her mind. Stubbornness is very bad in someone who has only bad ideas, but it's very good in someone who has good ideas. Luckily Fern is the smart kind of stubborn. And it can't be denied that Fern liked this plan especially because it would bring her to her grandmother, and Fern hadn't given up on the idea of finding a place that felt like home. Maybe she would find it there, Fern thought, in the house where her mother had grown up with the woman who'd raised her.

The Bone paced back and forth. "No, no. Eliza wouldn't leave the book with her mother. She wouldn't do that to me. Her mother can't stand me! And now the Miser, too! It's all wrong. All very, very wrong. I won't go. I won't do it!"

But Fern knew she was right. She knew she was very, very right. She looked at the Bone with her big eyes and she smiled. He sagged. And just then, from above, an accordion started up—happy, bouncy music—and the clogs set in like a hailstorm—hailstones the size of clogs. The Bone stared up at the ceiling then back at Fern, and Fern knew that the Bone knew the only other option was to stay where they were. She knew she'd won.

PART 3

THE HOUSE OF BOOKS

THE NOSE

THE BONE WAS DRIVING THE OLD JALOPY. FERN
sat next to his suitcase and her own bag in the backseat where the seat belt worked. The Bone was giving
instructions about the new identities he'd created for
himself and Fern, but it was hard to concentrate on
what he was saying because he'd turned himself into
an encyclopedia salesman. He was wearing a name tag
pinned to the lapel of a shabby green suit: HELLO! MY
NAME IS: MR. BIBB, SALES ASSOCIATE. His hair, which had
been a graying blond puff, was flat, black, and looked
shellacked, shiny as a Christmas ornament. Fern had pretended to be asleep in the morning while she listened to
him humming in the low baritone he'd used with Mr.

Harton. She heard him curse under his breath, and then he cheered, "Yes, yes, that's it!" Shortly thereafter, the house smelled of something sharp like paint. The smell reminded Fern of Mr. Drudger daubing and rubbing shoe polish into his loafers. Fern guessed that the Bone had tried to become a different person through the magical transformations based on *The Art of Being Anybody*. He'd failed, and resorted to faking it. Had he put shoe polish on his hair? Was that new bulbous nose made of rubber and glued on? And that smarmy little mustache?

The sloppy old car made Fern feel seasick, a queasiness that was aggravated by the watery sound of the Bone's new lisp, a Mr. Bibb trait he'd taken on. There were too many *s*'s in everything. "I'm Missster Bibb and you're Ida Bibb, my daughter. And we're jusst passssing through for a few weekss. We need a room for jussst that much time. We're heading wesst to visssit family. Jusst let me do the talking."

When Fern came up with the plan to look for the book at her grandmother's, she hadn't realized that she and the Bone couldn't show up as themselves on her doorstep. No, no, the Bone had convinced her that they'd each have to go as somebody else. This was disappointing because Fern had wanted to go to her grandmother's house to figure out if it felt like home. How could she do this if she was Ida Bibb? "But I sometimes blurt out weird things when I'm nervous," Fern said. "I do sometimes. My brain just rattles on like a train with too many cars, and then I find out I've just said something that doesn't make sense. What can I do about it? I can't do much. Can I?" It dawned on Fern that she wasn't saying all of this in her head. She was saying it out loud and that was a nice thing. Still she was nervous, and she pulled three barrettes from her pocket to lock down her wild hair.

"Think of milk. Think of a big glasss of milk. Sstop talking and try to conjure the biggesst, whitesst, creamiesst glasss of milk you can, all beaded with dropss of water. Try to make it clear in your head, like you could jusst reach into spacse and pick it up and drink it. Think of ssoup, cheesse, lemonss, appless, plumss. That'll keep your brain occupied."

"Do you have to talk like that?" Fern felt nauseous and thinking about milk, soup, cheese, lemons, apples, and plums wasn't helping matters.

"Yesss."

"I don't think she'll believe us! I don't think this'll work," Fern said. "You should ask her for the book. Maybe she knows she has it and will just hand it to you."

"Nothing further from the truth. That woman doessn't like me. She never did. Your mother told her that she'd reformed me, turned me into a real healer.

A good guy. But her mother wouldn't have much to do with me. 'He doessn't even like to read!' her mother would ssay, like that wass the greatesst sssin in the world. The only good thing isss that she didn't like the Missser either. She didn't like either of uss."

"Do you like to read?"

"I liked when your mother read to me. She read like a dream."

"I just have a feeling it's going to be strange," Fern said.

"It will."

"I've got a bad feeling."

"Today'ss a good day, Fern! It'ss a very good day. Thingss are already looking up."

"They are?"

He pulled the car over onto a grassy shoulder and stopped. Fern looked at the Bone. He said, "Look!

Look at my nosse."

"What?"

He pushed the squat nose, then pulled on it, then wiggled it around. It looked fat, real, completely attached. "That there iss the real McCoy, Fern, I tell you. I couldn't get any of the other sstuff right, but the nosse, that iss a genuine nossse, fully transsformed. I may be faking Mr. Bibb, but my nosse issn't. It'ss the firsst time in a long time that I ever got any of it right. I wass thinking of the Great Realdo. He'd helped me oncse before, when I wass wooing your mother. I wass thinking today the ssame way I wass thinking all those yearss ago: 'I need your help. Jusst an inch of your great sspirit. Help me, Great Realdo.' And it worked." He smiled. He reached behind and patted Fern on the head. It was a soft little pat, not a mushy pat, but it was just a little sweet. He sighed and looked out the front windshield. "There'ss the housse." He pointed

down a long dirt driveway to a tall yellow farmhouse and a large red barn surrounded by fields. There was a sign dug into the dirt: BOARDERS WELCOME. MUST BE TIDY AND WELL-READ.

The Bone gazed up at the house. He started humming the song Fern had heard him singing the night before. "Sweet, sweet, my sweet darling angel, where have you gone, where have you gone?" He put the car in gear and headed down the long, bumpy driveway.

Fern stuck her head out the window. She stared at the house. She figured it looked like a place she could call home; it was hard to tell, really, when she didn't know exactly what a place she could call home should look like. A wind kicked up, gusted. One of the shingles on the roof lifted in the breeze but didn't come off. Something white fluttered under the shingle, just for a moment, a quick flipping of what seemed like pages. Was the roof made of books? The Bone jerked the car to a stop in front of the house. Dust rose up, then settled. No, no, it was just an ordinary house, Fern assured herself, with an ordinary roof.

UNEXPECTED GUESTS

GRANDMOTHERS. AH, GRANDMOTHERS! THE world needs more of them, if you ask me. I'm quite nostalgic and overly sentimental about grandmothers. My own is a very short, yet gorgeous and ample Southern belle. Her house is filled with poodles and hand-guns—her second husband being a military man. She wears muu-muus year-round, drives only Cadillacs and adores Liberace—for his good taste. But Fern's grandmother isn't at all like my dear old granny. Fern had never met her real grandmother. She wondered what she would be like, and if there would be any traces left in the house from her mother, something, anything, that would tell Fern more about her. Fern wondered what she would find.

The Bone was carrying their bags and Fern had the banged-up umbrella. An old crumbly sidewalk that she hadn't noticed before ran from the street down the long driveway and ended right at the front door. It divided the thigh-high underbrush that rustled not too far away. Fern looked out at the tall grass and barbed weeds of the front yard. There were small boxes made of bricks sticking up here and there. They looked like chimneys, but on the ground and without smoke. Up the hill toward the main road, Fern thought she also saw some windows peeking out of the ground and latticework. It was confusing, and Fern was too jittery to try to make sense out of it. She was wary now of unfamiliar front yards since the last one had had a rooster man in it, not to mention spies.

The Bone knocked at the paint-chipped door. The door, latched by a chain, opened just a bit. Two eyes swam up below the chain. That's what Fern noticed first—the eyes behind a pair of round glasses that made the big eyes look even bigger. In fact, the eyes seemed unconnected to a face, like two fish in a set of fish bowls. The eyes worried Fern. If Mr. and Mrs. Drudger thought Fern's big eyes were a deformity, what would they think of this pair? Fern thought of Little Red Riding Hood—"Grandma, what big eyes you have!" It wasn't a comforting association, as you can imagine.

Big and blue, the eyes glowed like headlights on a Buick in the middle of the night. The rest of the face slowly came into focus—a small bony nose and a pink wrinkled mouth that was as small as a bow you'd paste on a poodle to make it look fancy. Fern narrowed her own eyes, out of practiced manners.

"Who is it now? Can't be too careful!" The old woman said this out loud, but it was the kind of thing that should have stayed in her head.

The Bone started in on the speech he'd practiced, his red nose bobbing. "I'm Missster Bibb and thiss iss my daughter, Ida. We've come for a room. Sssaw the ssign. I ssell encsssyclopediass."

"Well, don't just stand out there! Come in. Come in," the fish-eyed woman said, unlatching the chain. Then she looked past Fern and the Bone to the yard, distracted by something she saw there and didn't like. She hobbled past them into the yard. "Is that another little house they've dug? Blast it!" She shook her head and hobbled back. Fern's grandmother was a small, arthritic old woman. She sagged and wheezed like an old accordion as she shuffled. She was bent over so far that it was as if she were looking up at the Bone and Fern from the bottom of a hole, and Fern wasn't so tall herself. There was more rustling and then quiet.

"Well," the old woman said, looking at Fern and the Bone impatiently. "I didn't mind a few in my yard, just a few, but they've gotten so content over the years with their little routines and their manners. Edgy! Uptight! Always digging a new little house, here and there. But they've come from a hard place. Poor things. I don't like to upset them!"

Fern had no idea who she was talking about—animals digging in the yard? Was she saying that the brick stacks were in fact little chimneys? Was there some sort of little neighborhood built under the front yard?

Fern was trying to be Ida Bibb, but she didn't really know Ida Bibb very well, so she didn't know exactly how she should act. She only knew that Ida Bibb wouldn't ask the woman if she'd had any children, a daughter, for example, named something like Eliza, and what exactly was she like. No. Fern reminded herself: don't ask about that. You must be exactly like Ida Bibb. But then it dawned on Fern that her grandmother didn't know who Ida Bibb was any more than Fern did. For that matter, her grandmother didn't know Fern Drudger, and so Fern decided right there that she should be herself, except she wouldn't mention anything about daughters, her grandmother's daughter in particular. Fern knew this would be hard because the only thing she wanted to do was ask questions. Not being able to made Fern nervous, and when Fern feels nervous, the chatter begins in her head followed by the occasional blurting. She was thinking: *Do you have gophers? I hear gophers are hard for a yard. Do you have groundhogs? They'll ruin a yard too. That's what I've heard. I sure hope you don't have gophers or groundhogs! That would be a shame. And they'd ruin a garden!* But she was blurting too: "Do you have a garden? Do you use weed killer? Do you mulch?"

Much to Fern's surprise, however, her grandmother didn't appear to be shocked by the blurting. She was listening intently. And so Fern continued on, thinking and blurting at the same time now. In fact, she was giving a lively speech. She went on talking about gophers and groundhogs and gardens for a good while. At one point, she wandered into the subject of being tender to a garden, raising it with love, like a, like a—but Fern did not say daughter. She said, "Well, like a garden. That's all." And she forged on with talk of shrubbery. The Drudgers and their neighbors often talked about lawns and yards and such, and although Fern had never seen either a gopher or a groundhog—both of which would have struck panic in her old neighborhood—she found herself unable to get off the track for fear of talking about her own mother. Eventually, mercifully, she simply ran out of breath.

And her grandmother said, "Yes, dear, to question (a): It's quite expansive. No to question (b). And a few years back to question (c). Never is the answer to question (d). . . ." And so on, until the old woman, quite incomprehensibly, had answered all of Fern's questions.

But for some reason, it made Fern feel much better. Did it make her feel at home? No, not really. She still didn't feel herself, but she did find her grandmother reassuring in a way she couldn't explain.

"May I take your umbrella?" her grandmother asked. "It looks like it's seen better days."

Fern handed her the crumpled umbrella, and the old woman ushered them into the parlor. Fern was anxious to see inside the house that she might be able to call home. And here she was. The room was lit with small reading lamps and there were books everywhere, piled on the coffee table, under the coffee table, on the sofa and under it, too. Books were stacked up the stairs, and through the hall. Fern could see a small forest of books in the kitchen, books stacked on the table, the counters, like dishes in the dish rack. The rolltop desk (not rolled up) seemed to be belching books. Books lined every wall so that you couldn't see the walls at all. In fact, a mirror had been hung over the books as if the wall were made of books. And the oil paintings, which hung over the stacked books, depicted books. One was a still life of a bowl, but it was almost as if the fruit that was supposed to be in the bowl had been taken out and replaced with books. There were even books fitted in the rafters and hung in the hat rack's arms. This made it especially tricky for the old woman to find a spot to hang Fern's umbrella, but she fussed with it this way

and that, rearranging books until she had the umbrella hung and the books balancing just so.

Now, it's an odd thing to go inside some people's houses. Have you ever been house hunting? Well, I bet you haven't because sometimes I forget how young you are—which is a compliment, meaning you seem so mature for your age. Let me explain: house hunting isn't as exciting as it sounds. There is no actual "hunt." You don't hide out in the underbrush wearing camouflage and making noises like a house to lure the house into an open field. No, it's more like you go through house after house following around some sharply dressed someone who smells very mouthwashy, while they turn on and off light switches and ceiling fans, pointing out closet space while diverting your attention away from foundation cracks. But, while house hunting, you do realize that you're walking into somebody's private space, and it's an odd thing to suddenly know so much about a stranger—their bad taste in furnishings, their obsession with cow knickknacks, their overconfidence in the power of duct tape or certain rotten presidents. Now this house, *this house*, topped them all! It was clearly the house of someone who lived quite differently from the rest of society. Quite differently, indeed! It's the kind of house that no one could ever imagine buying because it so clearly belongs to one person and one person only in the whole wide world. Or, well, maybe two . . . because the house reminded Fern of her own bedroom, or at least the bedroom she was trying to create with her ten-cent yard-sale books.

Although it was a wonderful thing to be surrounded by books, Fern felt overwhelmed. There were so very, very many books! Her eyes darted from title to title. And weren't Fern and the Bone here to find a book? How in the world could that be possible with so very many books? Fern suddenly, deeply, missed her old bedroom, and she wondered how Howard was making out and if her lichen was still growing in her closet. No, Fern decided, she didn't feel at home here. It was just too much!

The old woman said, "First things first. An introduction. I've got your names, but what would you like to call me?"

The Bone looked at Fern in a way that seemed to say, *I told you she was a strange one.*

Fern shrugged. "I don't know. What did your parents name you?"

"That was so long ago, it's hard to say, really."

"Don't you have it written down?" Fern asked.

"Why most certainly," the old woman said, glancing around. "I must have written it somewhere. Somewhere." The old woman grabbed a book off the shelf. "Books," she said, and she held it open and shook it.

124

The pages flapped back and forth. "Look at this. Nothing!" She pulled another one off the shelf and shook it, too. "Nothing ever falls out anymore. Now a giant was hard to get out. Sure, you could shake a boot loose, but it'd take a whole day to get a giant out of a book, and what to do with him once he's out? And how to get him back, even if he wants to go back?" She handed a book to the Bone. "Shake this one, Mr. Bibb. Go ahead. Maybe you'll have better luck."

The Bone shook the book and nothing came out. He handed it back to the old woman, who seemed victorious, as if the Bone was proving her point. "See? See what I'm talking about? The little creatures used to slip right out, especially the ones who were looking for something. But aren't we all looking for something?" She glanced at Fern and the Bone with a kindly twinkle in her eye—or was it a menacing glint? Hard to say. Fern, for one, didn't know. All she knew was that the old woman wasn't making sense at all.

Fern was getting really nervous. She didn't want to start talking. She could feel words bubbling up again, *You might think I'm after something, but you'd be wrong. . . .* She tried to think of milk, as the Bone had suggested. She tried to think of cheese, then soup, then lemons, apples and plums. "How about Mrs. Appleplum? We could call you that. It's a nice name."

"Yes," the old woman said. "Mrs. Appleplum will do just fine. Tell the new guest upstairs to call me Mrs. Appleplum, if you see him. He just arrived this morning with an enormous black trunk and bulky sack, and he didn't want to name me anything. He said he'd call me ma'am, since I refused to give him a name. He's a whiskery fellow who told me that he likes his quiet and privacy. Do you all like your privacy? It sure has been a busy day here. I usually don't have any guests. And since these books are nothing but books again, after all these years, pages and bindings and glue, well, most of the little characters have run off. Except those messing in the yard, digging, digging—and a few little thieves. If something's missing, come to me straightaway. The house has its little thieves." The old woman's large eyes toured the book-packed walls. She'd lost her train of thought, it seemed, or more like the train had derailed. She said, "I'll get tea. The water's already hot." With this, Mrs. Appleplum limped out of the room, hunched like a question mark.

Fern and the Bone stared at each other. The Bone looked ashen, with beads of sweat on his forehead. "There are more books, Fern! I didn't think it could happen, but she's gotten more books! How will we ever find the one we need?"

"Do you think the guest is the Miser?" Fern asked.

"SSHHH!" the Bone said. "Of course, he is! Gosh, I'm hot. It's hot in here, like a furnace. She's gotten old, Fern. Much older than ever. How could she have gotten so old? Has that much time passed by? And the Miser is here!"

"This is good! Can't you see it's working?" Fern said, excited that her plan was taking shape.

"It's like an oven in here. Don't you think? Hot, hot, hot." He sighed, stuffing one hand in the pocket of his sport coat so that his elbow stuck out, like someone in the middle of singing, "I'm a little teapot . . ."

Fern kept staring at him because his nose, which had been chubby and fat and red, was shrinking. It was thinning out, narrowing to the Bone's naturally small nub. "Your nose!" Fern said. "Your . . . your nose!"

The Bone grabbed his nose. "No! No!" he said. "I can't believe this!" He stared up at the ceiling, chiding himself, "Get it together, Bone! Get it together!"

"It's okay," Fern said. She could hear Mrs. Apple-plum in the kitchen, the ping of spoons on china. "Don't panic. Do you have a hankie?"

He nodded, pulling a crumpled one from a back pocket of his ugly polyester suit slacks—Mr. Bibb, it turned out, shopped at low-end discount stores.

"Keep sneezing," Fern said. "I'll distract her! And don't forget your lisp!"

127

Mrs. Appleplum walked in and served them tea. Each cup handle had a string wrapped around it with a note that read: DRINK ME. Maybe you know the book about Alice, a girl who fell down a rabbit hole? Well, Fern thought of her right away, the fact that when the girl drank things labeled DRINK ME, she shrank.

"Are you going to drink it?" Mrs. Appleplum asked.

"Am I? I guess so. It says to drink it," said Fern.

"Are you afraid to drink it?" Mrs. Appleplum asked.

"Do you mean, am I afraid I'll shrink or something?"

"Humph!" Mrs. Appleplum said, a little disappointed. "Well, well. I didn't know you'd pass that test." Fern hadn't known it had been a test. Mrs. Appleplum looked up with her bulgy fish eyes at Fern. "The sign at the end of the driveway says 'Must be well read.' I have my ways of finding these things out. There's nothing worse than a poor reader." And here she glared at the Bone, dressed as Mr. Bibb, hiding behind his hankie. She looked at him sharply, as if maybe she knew he wasn't Mr. Bibb at all.

The Bone sneezed. "Dusst! I'm allergic to dusst!" the Bone said. "Can we take the tea up to our room to drink? It'ss been a long day!"

"Fine. Follow me."

Mrs. Appleplum lead the way up the staircase, narrowed by books. The hallway was lined with books too. Fern was dizzied by all of the books. How would they ever find the one book they needed. . . how in the world?

When they passed the first door, Mrs. Appleplum put her finger to her pink poodle-bow lips to remind them that the whiskery guest preferred quiet. Fern passed by the closed door slowly. She listened hard and thought she heard a small scratching noise, then a cough, then nothing.

Mrs. Appleplum opened the second door. "Here's your room. One room. The two of you will have to share," she said. The room was small, book-cluttered, with two single beds separated by a small nightstand. Mrs. Appleplum cleared her throat. Her eyes got a bit glassy. "It used to be my daughter's room, but she's gone now. She passed away."

Fern's throat cinched tight. She thought she might cry. "I'm sorry to hear that," Fern said, but she said it too convincingly. She said it with too much love. Mrs. Appleplum looked at her oddly. Fern busied herself with the room. She realized she was hoping it smelled of lilacs. She remembered the Bone telling her that her mother always smelled of that sweet perfume. But too much time had passed, Fern guessed. The room only smelled of books.

"It's a nice room," Fern said. But really it was hard

129

to tell if it was a nice room. It was a dark room, because books were lined up blocking the one window that would have given a nice view of the front yard, the old jalopy, the red barn and the long driveway to the road. Fern tried not to think about it, but she couldn't help herself; this was her mother's bedroom, her mother's! On the wall facing the bed was a painting—yes, hung in front of a wall stacked with books—of goldfish in a small pond, and she imagined that when her mother used to lie down at night, that painting is what she saw—plump goldfish trolling the water, the lily pads lush, purple, dreamy. Fern couldn't think about it anymore. She could feel herself wanting to blurt questions at Mrs. Appleplum about her daughter. A million questions.

Fern turned her attention to the Bone. It was clear he didn't want to think about Mrs. Appleplum's daughter, either. He was trying desperately to stay in character. He'd already lost his nose! He flicked the light switch off and on, a test, and wiggled the bedroom doorknob. He opened a closet door. It was bricked solid with books. He opened the dresser drawers—more books.

"Where will we put our clothesss?" he asked.

"On your body, of course!" Mrs. Appleplum responded, as if the Bone were dense.

Now Fern's stomach lurched. *The Art of Being*

Anybody could be anywhere! What if it had fallen behind a row of books? What if it was hidden inside another, bigger book?

"You can pay me for two weeks, up front," Mrs. Appleplum said. "Put the money in an envelope and leave it on the kitchen table."

The Bone sneezed and nodded.

Mrs. Appleplum was going over house rules. "No extra guests. Only quick showers. Breakfast at 8 A.M. Lunch on your own. Dinner at 6 P.M. Sharp. Always sharp." Fern started picking up books—*The Rules of Baseball* and *Salsa Recipes*. She picked up a third book off the table. It was leather bound with no words on the cover. *Maybe it's this one,* she thought. She had to start somewhere. Fern turned to the first page, but, no, this one was called *The Official Book of Fairies*. Mrs. Appleplum was still going: "Watch out while walking the grounds. A fellow from the insurance company fell down a rabbit hole and was lost for some time." She stopped, glancing around the room, as if she'd forgotten something, something. "Oh, and there's one more thing . . . ," she said. "What was it now? What was it?" Her eyes found the painting and then opened wide—I should say *wider*, since her eyes were always wide. "Oh, yes!" She pointed her finger in the air and then at the painting.

"Don't feed the goldfish, please!"

Fern and the Bone looked around for a fishbowl, then their eyes came back to the painting.

"In the painting?" Fern asked. "Don't feed the goldfish in the painting?"

"Yes," Mrs. Appleplum answered. "Please don't. If you do, they'll only grow used to it and forget how to take care of themselves!" She turned to go, adding over her shoulder, "And don't pick the lilies off the lily pad either! I like them just the way they are!"

3

THE WINK

"SHE'S STRANGE," THE BONE SAID AS HE AFFIXED
a bulbous fake nose from a kit he'd brought with him for
just such an emergency of failing confidence. He was
pasting and readjusting while looking into a small mirror, which stood on a dresser he'd found behind some
stacked books. "Sometimes I think her brain is made of
pie filling. Did you notice how she just prattles on and
then walks off? Odd. The whole place is strange. I
warned you, didn't I? And her name is Dora, Dorathea
Gretel. Why wouldn't she just use her real name?"

"We didn't," Fern said, thinking of the name Eliza
Gretel, her mother's name when she was Fern's age.

"Yes, well, but, you know . . ."

"What do you think is living in the yard?"

"Could be anything!" the Bone answered.

Fern pushed her suitcase against the foot of the bed. She set her tea on a stack of books on the nightstand. She glanced at the painting of the fat goldfish. She suddenly had the intense desire to try to reach her hand inside of it, run her hand around in the water, maybe even throw bread crumbs to the goldfish and pick one of the lilies from the lily pads. Has it ever happened to you that you had no desire to do something until someone told you not to? *Don't poke your finger into the cake!* your mother tells you, and although it hadn't dawned on you to poke your finger into the cake, you suddenly want to do it, desperately. This was Fern's thinking, and she was above it. I'm not above it. I'd poke my finger in the cake *and* I'd try to reach into the painting, but not Fern. She's tougher than that and she had a mission.

She started pulling books off of piles. "We've got to start looking! No time to waste!" She picked up a safari book, a medical book, and *The World of Bats*. This one she put in a special spot beside her bed. She wanted to look at it later. She wondered if she'd learn something about bats, probably not that they could turn into marbles at indoor swimming pools, but something.

The Bone was pacing in the narrow alley between the beds. "I want to see the other guest. I want to look

134

him in the eye and wink. If he winks back, well, then, case closed. It's him all right."

"Not exactly case closed. Some people wink back if you wink at them, you know. The new guest could be an ordinary person." (Didn't I tell you Fern was smart?)

"Hmm," the Bone said. "Well, the wink will point us in the right direction."

Fern looked around the room. She was trying to imagine her mother as a young girl, Fern's own age. "Do you think my mother liked it here?"

The Bone stopped pacing. He ran his hand over the lamp shade. He sat down on the bed and placed his hand tenderly on the pillow. "Yes, yes."

"Could she shake books?"

"She could do much, much more. She could do almost anything. She was a wonder!" He looked over at the window. "I once leaned a ladder against this house. Right up to that window. It was the Great Realdo who'd helped me then, too. That was the other time I called on him. A butterfly appeared. It led me to the ladder and perched on my shoulder. It stayed there. Eliza appeared at the window. She climbed down the ladder with me, and the butterfly disappeared. Off we went. I saw the butterfly again, just before they called me out of the prison yard. It sat on my shoulder that time too. I thought it would be good news, but it had come to comfort me. The Great

135

Realdo." His eyes pooled with tears, but he didn't cry.

Fern gazed at the painting. She imagined how cool the water would feel. "Why didn't her mother like you, really, why?"

"Even though Eliza wanted to go with me, well, her mother wanted her to stay. She had big plans for her daughter, I guess, better than settling down with a mischief maker like me."

Just then there was a loud noise, a cross between a bang and a thump. It came from down the hall. It made Fern jump, but the Bone didn't notice it at all. He'd started humming that song again: "Sweet, sweet, my sweet darling angel . . ."

"The Miser!" Fern said. "You know, I think I should be the one to see him first, not you. You're emotional about him and I'm not. I mean, I've never met him. Maybe I can get more information from him. He might be nice to me. Polite. He might politely answer questions."

The Bone didn't seem to want to be pulled away from his dreaminess. "I guess," he said eventually, not sounding too convinced.

"How about I go open his door and tell him I thought it was the bathroom."

The Bone nodded, cautiously. "But be careful!" he said. "Be very careful!"

Fern walked out the bedroom door and down the

hall, but she stopped abruptly when she saw a man walk out of the first bedroom. He had a key and was locking his door. He was a tall, thin man with gray bushy hair.

"Excuse me, I was on my way to the bathroom. Do you know . . ." she said, and the man turned toward her. He had a white beard, mustache, and enormous eyebrows that hung down over his eyes. In fact, she couldn't see his eyes at all, which distracted her. "Did you hear a loud noise?"

The Miser nodded. "I was killing a spider with a book," he said in a grim whisper.

"Oh," Fern said. And then because she couldn't think of anything else, she said, "Mrs. Appleplum told us to tell you that she wants to be called Mrs. Appleplum."

"Who's Mrs. Appleplum?"

"Well, that would be Mrs. Appleplum. You know, the woman who runs the house. I'm Ida Bibb. I'm staying here with my father, Mr. Bibb, who sells encyclopedias."

"Very original."

"Thank you," Fern said, though it was obviously not a compliment. "What's your name?"

"Mr. Haiserblaitherness."

It was an obviously fake name. She wanted to say *Very original!* but didn't want to make him angry. "What do you do?" Fern asked.

"I'm busy. I don't have time to talk to children."

He was about to leave, but then he turned back to Fern. "Be careful of the spiders. The one I killed was poisonous. You wouldn't want to be bitten and die in the night."

"No, no," Fern said, standing there awkwardly.

"The bathroom is in the opposite direction," he said.

"Thanks," Fern said, and she gave a wink, just a little quick one. But if Mr. Haiserblaitherness winked back, Fern couldn't see it under his enormous eyebrows.

Mr. Haiserblaitherness walked away, turning down the stairs. Fern ran back to her room. She ran to the window, pulling down the books, and opened it wide.

"What happened?" the Bone asked.

Fern didn't say a word. She looked out at the yard. Two rabbits seemed to be chatting together like old friends—was one of them wearing a blue jacket and the other white gloves? Could that be right? They hopped away as soon as the front door slammed. Mr. Haiserblaitherness marched out, cutting across the yard. Fern knew he was the Miser. She just knew. Some people just know things. I'm not one of them. The first time I heard The Beatles, I said, "Oh, they'll never last." I thought that the slogan "Pork, the other white meat," would revolutionize the pork industry. I thought by now we'd be flying everywhere in motorized jet-backpacks. But Fern isn't like me, or most people for that matter. She really can just know things, and she knew she was watching the Miser. He was heading to the barn.

"You don't think . . . ," Fern whispered.

"What?" the Bone asked.

Mr. Haiserblaitherness lifted the barn door's latch and swung open the barn's wide hinged doors, and there, right there before him, was a solid wall of books. The barn was packed tight. Fern and the Bone watched Mr. Haiserblaitherness curse and spit, his whole body shaking with anger. He kicked the ground, his shoes pawing the dirt until a thin cloud of dust rose up and, when it settled, the only thing standing there was an angry, snorting bull.

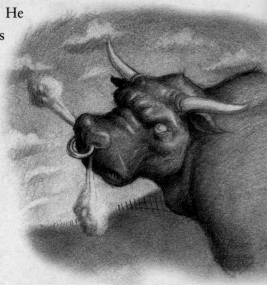

THE TEST

THE KITCHEN HAD PATHS RUNNING THROUGH the stacked books. Mrs. Appleplum zipped around the maze. Fern and the Bone were sitting at the kitchen table. The Bone slowly, gently pushed a tower of books that sat in the middle of the table to one side so he and Fern could see each other. There were four places set, but no sign of the Miser.

The grandfather clock bonged six times, and it was clear that Mrs. Appleplum wasn't going to wait for the Miser to arrive. She buzzed over to the stove and back to the table. "I've got more tests!" she said, smiling at Fern. "More tests for Ida Bibb! Are you ready?"

Fern almost didn't recognize her name—Ida Bibb? But after a second's hesitation and a small kick from the Bone under the table, she piped up, "Oh, yes! Yes!"

"First, we'll begin simply," Mrs. Appleplum said. The kitchen was hot from the hardworking stove. A moist steam made some of the books look puffy. Mrs. Appleplum's cheeks were flushed. She uncovered a dish with a flourish.

The eggs were under-fried. Their greasy yolks jiggled. They were dyed a bright, bright green, like the ham. This was easy. Fern knew all of the Dr. Seuss books, all the silly rhyming, the furry, skinny-legged creatures. "No thank you," Fern said. "I do not like green eggs and ham."

The Bone said, "I'll passs too," but it was obvious that Mrs. Appleplum didn't care about *his* likes and dislikes. Fern had gotten the answer right. Mrs. Appleplum buzzed away and back again. This time she held out a dish with four pieces of wrapped bubble gum. "Your entire meal!" she said. "It will taste like an entire meal, one course after the next!"

The Bone picked up a piece and began to unwrap it. "Really? That'sss amazing," he said. "Where did you get thisss?"

Fern swiped it out of his hands and placed it back on the tray.

"No thanks. I'm afraid that I might turn into a blueberry if I ate this for dinner."

Maybe you know about a boy named Charlie who won a trip through a chocolate factory owned and operated by Willy Wonka and about a certain Violet Beauregarde who loved bubble gum much too much for anyone's good health.

Mrs. Appleplum smiled, whizzing back through the maze of books.

The Bone whispered, "Hey, I would have liked to have tried that!"

Mrs. Appleplum appeared again. "That leaves me only with this." She whisked off another lid. "Turkish Delight!"

Now this was hard to resist. It was a beautiful Jell-O-like extravaganza covered with powdered sugar. Fern could smell the sugar and rose water. The Bone had already lifted his plate, hoping someone would fill it up. "I cssertainly am getting a real appetite!" he said.

Fern looked up at Mrs. Appleplum. Fern was thinking of a book in which kids had walked into a wardrobe and gotten into quite a bit of trouble in another world altogether. She said, "That would be lovely, but I'm afraid, very afraid, that once I started eating it, I wouldn't be able to stop."

Mrs. Appleplum looked at Fern like Fern was a pearl, a shiny pearl that she had just found in an oyster. "Very well done! Very well done! How about grilled

143

cheese and tomato soup?"

Fern thought about it. She traced and retraced her mind. Grilled cheese? Tomato soup? She turned to the Bone. He was looking at her pleadingly. "Okay," she said. "That sounds fine."

And so, that was it. Mrs. Appleplum had given up. She was sweaty and seemed very happy in her defeat this time. She said, "And you can lick the wallpaper, too, if you'd like. The limes taste like limes." And she walked back to the stove.

The Bone looked at Fern, then at the wallpaper. Only a small sliver of it—limes, cherries, oranges—was showing, what with all of the books. She shrugged, and they both leaned in close to the wallpaper, cautiously inspecting it. "You go," Fern said.

"No, you," the Bone said.

"Both at the same time," Fern offered.

The Bone licked an orange. Fern licked a lime.

"Lime!" Fern said.

"Orange!" the Bone said.

Fern was really starting to get the idea of this place. When Mrs. Appleplum returned with soup and sandwiches and glasses of milk, Fern was ready to turn the tables. The Bone started slurping and munching, but Fern was eating slowly. She had questions for Mrs. Appleplum.

"Would there happen to be a peach tree around

here?" she asked casually.

"Yes," said Mrs. Appleplum, dipping her sandwich in her soup.

"And is one of the peaches . . . oversized?"

"Yes. You could even call it a giant peach," said Mrs. Appleplum, chewing.

"I've noticed, too, that the sidewalk ends right at your front door. Any comment?"

"No, no comment. That is where the sidewalk ends. That's all. But if I were to pack up and take off, I wouldn't pack a suitcase."

Fern paused a minute. She was thinking . . . what else would you pack your things in? And then she remembered those two kids who ran away and didn't want anyone to know, so they had to be tricky. "Would you pack a violin case?"

"Of course!" Mrs. Appleplum said.

"And those thieves you said filled this house, they aren't little *people* are they? They aren't Borrowers, are they?"

"Could be."

"Then, let me guess, those creatures digging in the garden aren't gophers."

"Nope."

"Hobbits? Are they hobbits who are living in your front yard, who have good manners and are uptight and come from a hard place?" Fern asked.

Mrs. Appleplum beamed. She looked at the Bone. "Do you know what we have here, Mr. Bibb? Do you have any idea?"

The Bone's mouth was too full to speak. He shook his head and wiped his cheesy mustache.

Mrs. Appleplum shook her head and smiled and smiled. "Oh, my!" she said. "No, you don't have any idea, Mr. Bibb. No idea. Oh, my. Oh, my!" And she dabbed her teary cheeks.

Then the stairs creaked. The Bone's back straightened. Mrs. Appleplum blew her nose. Fern watched a shadow flash through the living room and then saw the full, dark shape of the Miser, dressed as Mr. Haiserblaitherness with his bushy eyebrows hiding his eyes. He was wearing a large hat that puffed out on his head like a chef's hat, but it wasn't a chef's hat. It was black and velvety. He looked haggard, exhausted, worn-out. "Good evening," he said.

The Bone stood up stiffly, turned and saw the Miser there. The Bone was staring intently at the Miser's face. "Nicsse to meet you, Mr. Haiserblaitherness," the Bone said.

"Yes, nice to meet you too. And what was your name again?"

"Mr. Bibb and my daughter, Ida."

Fern smiled.

"Yes, lovely girl," the Miser said blandly. Fern noticed

that the Miser seemed to be a bit breathless, and there was a mark on the tip of his nose, a small extra hole, as if the tip of his nose had been pierced . . . like a bull's. Fern thought of the cloud that was hiding in the neighbor's bushes and how the man from the census bureau had one hand made of cloud. It seemed to her that the Miser wasn't always perfect at getting himself from one disguise to another, quickly and completely.

"You missed dinner, Mr. Haiserblaitherness. We start at six o'clock sharp!" Mrs. Appleplum told him.

"And I don't care for hats worn indoors. It isn't well-mannered."

"Oh," said the Miser, "oh, wèll, let me take my leave then. I won't disturb you." He bowed and left, but never took off his hat.

THE SPIDER

"HORNS," FERN WHISPERED TO THE BONE AS they did the dishes. "Horns, don't you think that's what he's got under his hat?"

"It could happen. The effects of a transformation could linger, but not for long. In the morning he'll be back fully. But he'll be tired. That kind of transformation takes a lot of energy. He'll need to sleep." The Bone was washing and Fern was drying. The dishes had to be put back into the cupboards because there was no place to let them sit and dry. Books were everywhere. In fact, books lined the back of the cupboard, leaving only enough room for the four dishes. Silverware was kept in mugs on the counter, because the drawers were all filled with books, too.

Fern rubbed the dishes in quick circles. She was thinking hard. "But I don't think he wanted to turn into a bull when he got angry seeing all of those books in the barn. It seems to me that you and the Miser have opposite problems. You can't make the transformation, and he can't stop himself from making the transformation," Fern said. "Right?"

"I guess you're right," the Bone said as he turned off the faucet. "We should go through the rest of the books in our room. I think we can finish them off tonight."

"But there's got to be an easier way," Fern told him. "There must be some kind of short cut! We could search our whole lives and never find *The Art of Being Anybody*!"

As they walked through the parlor, passing Fern's mangled black umbrella still hanging precariously from the hat rack, Mrs. Appleplum stopped them. She was sitting on the sofa under a glass globe light, doing some hand-stitching. This surprised Fern, because she expected Mrs. Appleplum to read in every second of her spare time. Mrs. Appleplum poked the needle through the cloth she was working on, and propped her glasses up on her head. She rubbed her eyes. "Mr. Bibb, I was wondering if I could borrow Ida for a little bit. My eyes are so tired, I was hoping she could read to me."

They exchanged glances. Fern had planned on going through as many books as she could and also on stealing some time to write in her diary. But they both knew that Mrs. Appleplum might hold the best clues of all.

"Of courssse," the Bone told her. "Absssolutely."

So the Bone headed upstairs, and Fern sat down on the sofa next to Mrs. Appleplum.

"Here," the old woman said, "these three." She handed Fern three books.

"Which one do you want me to read?" Fern asked.

"One? No, no, all three, please. One line at a time from each. I prefer to read three at a time. It's more interesting."

"But, but, how can you keep it straight if you read one sentence from one, then the next, then the next? It's too confusing."

"Well," said Mrs. Appleplum, "it takes practice. But I suppose there are those who find playing one game of chess fully consuming, and then there was that fellow Bobby Fischer, who could play a dozen games at once, keeping them all in his head."

This seemed to make sense to Fern. Mrs. Appleplum was a quarter of the way into each book—*Anne Frank: The Diary of a Young Girl; Fair and Tender Ladies;* and *Catherine, Called Birdy.* While Mrs. Appleplum stitched, Fern read a sentence from each one, in turn. At first she concentrated so hard that it seemed like her head might explode, but slowly, slowly, she let go. She let things sink in, and it seemed she was getting the hang of it. In fact, it seemed like the three books had a lot in common. They were all about young girls writing down their own lives in diaries and letters. The stories swirled into one another and around in Fern's head.

Finally, Mrs. Appleplum said, "That's good, Ida. You can stop there."

"Are you sure? I can keep going if you want."

"No, no. That's fine. Do you like the books?"

"I do. I think all the girls are very smart."

"Well, I think that most smart young girls like to write things down. Don't you?"

"I do." Fern looked at what Mrs. Appleplum was sewing. It was a tiny dress, only big enough for a very small doll. Fern hoped that her staring at it would invite Mrs. Appleplum to make a comment, explain the little dress, but Mrs. Appleplum didn't say a word about it.

"Good night, Ida."

"Good night."

Fern walked up the narrow stairs, passed slowly by the Miser's room, pausing long enough to hear his mysterious scratching noises. She heard a soft hum from her bedroom door, and she knew what it was right away—the Bone with his "Sweet, sweet, my sweet darling angel, where have you gone, where have you gone?" Fern pretended to trip in the hallway. "Ouch!" she said loudly. "Darn it!" And the humming stopped. She opened the door, sat on the bed and rubbed her shin.

"Are you okay?" the Bone asked.

"I'm fine. Just caught my shin on the edge of a book."

"That's a hazard in this house."

"You betcha," Fern said.

"I've looked at every book in this room, some twice. Nothing. I'm tired," the Bone said. "This trip has taken more out of me than I expected."

"I'm tired, too," said Fern, and she was. Reading three books at the same time had taken its toll. So, they got ready for bed—one brushing teeth while the other got dressed in pajamas. Soon, they were both in their beds.

"Sweet dreams," the Bone said.

"Sweet dreams," said Fern. She took the barrettes out of her hair. It felt good to have her hair loose on her head.

Shortly the Bone was snoring, deep rattling breaths. But Fern couldn't sleep although she was sleepy. She climbed out of bed and dug her diary out of her bag. There was a small breeze and a stream of moonlight coming in through the open window, where they'd cleared away the books to spy on the Miser. She sat down, untied the small key from around her neck and opened the diary. She had so much to catch up on—her grandmother and this house of books and the Miser turning into a bull. But as soon as Fern opened the diary, there was the picture of her mother. She was careful with the photograph. She held it delicately by its edges—her mother, her round belly, her big eyes, her soft smile. For the first time, Fern noticed the background of the picture. Fern wrote what she saw in the photograph:

It looks like a gas station, an old gas station with ancient-looking pumps, maybe so old they were already abandoned even back then. There's a record player behind my mother, on a small table, its cord winding back through the gas station's door. And my mother's skirt is off to one side, as if she'd been caught swaying or slowly dancing.

Her mind drifted back to Mrs. Appleplum, and she

wrote down what Mrs. Appleplum looked like and all about the house. She wrote everything she could think of—even what the Miser had said about killing a spider—all the way up to what Mrs. Appleplum had just said to Fern while reading the books: *Well, I think that most smart young girls like to write things down. Don't you?*

Then Fern thought to herself: *Don't you? Most smart young girls write things down. Write things down.*

Fern sat upright in bed.

A diary! Her mother had kept a diary! She'd written down things she'd seen, things she'd thought were important. *Just like I do,* Fern thought, *like me!* It was something she and her mother had in common, and the idea thrilled her. Then it dawned on Fern that her mother must have written about *The Art of Being Anybody* in her diary. She turned to the Bone and whispered sharply, "Bone, Bone! Wake up!" The Bone didn't budge. Fern put the picture back in her diary, locked it and put the key on its string, retying it like a necklace.

When Fern looked over at the Bone again—he was still snoring—she saw a horrid sight. In the thin moonlight there was a spider, a big, black, hairy spider swaying on a silver line of webbing. Now Fern usually liked spiders, because of Charlotte, the wonderful, literate spider in that book about the pig and the girl named Fern, who wasn't named after a plastic plant made in China. But this spider didn't look like Charlotte at all. This spider dangled above the Bone's head. It had a shiny red belly, and Fern heard the Miser's voice in her head, *You wouldn't want to be bitten and die in the night*. It was a very, very big spider. Fern wondered if it could be the Miser. If he could change into a bull, he could probably just as easily turn into a spider. Could the Miser want to kill the Bone, right now in his bed?

The spider seemed to have inched closer to the Bone, its hairy pincers clicking. Fern was too scared to move, but she couldn't let the spider bite the Bone, her father. He was too precious to her now. She needed him more than she'd known. Fern's heart was knocking in her chest. She picked up a book beside her bed—*The Complete Guide to Fairies*. It was a heavy book. She would throw it at the spider and kill it. Fern took a fake practice throw, still holding tight to the book but aiming, and then another. The book was suddenly heavy, heavier than when she first picked it up. She lifted the book up and down quickly, testing its weight, and, then, much to her surprise, something slipped out of the book and landed on the wood floor with a small thud. Fern was shocked. She almost screamed. Fern saw a little fairy, a redheaded fairy, who would fit in the palm of your hand. The fairy had obviously been in the bath, and had only had enough time to grab a towel, which she wrapped around herself, startled and shaken, maybe a little embarrassed. You can't blame her. Wouldn't you be embarrassed if you slid out of the tub onto somebody's floor? Her hair was still sudsy. The fairy got up quickly, tried to look dignified, but then ran off, out the bedroom door.

As wild as this was, Fern had the power to shake things from books! Fern had to stay focused. The poisonous spider was still there, pincers and all. Not wanting any more fairies to pop out, Fern reached for another book. It was the perfect book! She knew exactly which book it was. She'd put it there earlier. She was so happy with her luck that she grabbed it as quickly as she could: *The World of Bats*. Yes! Of course! Bats eat spiders. That would fix things perfectly. She thought that a bat might snap from the book, flutter around the room once, then swoop at the spider, eat it and flap out the window.

Unfortunately, things don't always go as one hopes they will, even when the plan is a very smart one. You see, the Bone had shuffled through Fern's books, double-checking them, while she'd been reading to Mrs. Appleplum. Fern opened the book in the direction of the spider and shook it, just once, firmly. But instead of a bat, there was a small breeze that jostled the spider. Then gusts. The teacups, with their DRINK ME labels, started to rattle. Books flipped open, pages flapped, the lamp shade popped off its bulb. And then there was a swirling, swirling wind.

"What? What?" The Bone woke up with a start.

"TORNADO!" Fern called out, her blankets being sucked up into the funnel swirling around the room. Her pillow, too. "TORNADO!"

Fern and the Bone were gripping on to their mattresses now. There was pounding at the bedroom door. "IDA! MR. BIBB!" It was Mrs. Appleplum's voice. "WHAT IS IT? LET ME IN!"

Fern was now clawing to stay on her mattress. The tornado was pulling her up, up. The Bone was reaching for her. "TAKE MY HAND!" he yelled. They reached and reached, and finally the Bone grabbed hold of her hand, but now it was the only thing keeping her from disappearing into the funnel, which bumped around the room violently. Fern's fingers were slipping. "I CAN'T HOLD ON!" she yelled.

Just then Mrs. Appleplum busted into the room. The door hit the tornado like a lever at the bottom of a pinball machine and smacked it—spider and all— out the window.

Mrs. Appleplum looked around the wind-kicked room. Books were still dropping onto the floor, the bed.

The covers landed in a lump, sagging over the dresser. "What happened?"

"I think I killed Mr. Haiserblaitherness!" said Fern.

"Are you okay?" the Bone said. "Are you okay?"

"I'm fine. But I think I KILLED Mr. Haiserblaitherness!"

"What, child?" said Mrs. Appleplum. "No, you haven't. He's right here."

And there at her side, the Miser appeared. The hole in his nose was gone now. He was breathing normally, and his hat was off too, revealing a normal, hornless head.

"I . . . I . . . I shook a book, by accident, not knowing . . ."

Everyone was staring at Fern.

"And. . . ," urged Mrs. Appleplum, as if she knew exactly what was going to come next.

"Well, a fairy fell out of the first one. But there was a spider, a poisonous spider, so I thought I'd get the book on bats so the bat could eat the spider. But it wasn't a book on bats. It was something else."

"Oh, my," said Mrs. Appleplum. She stared at Fern intently. "Little girl! Do you know what you've done?"

Fern looked at the Bone—who was pale and swallowing dryly—and at the Miser, who glared, then to Mrs. Appleplum again.

"You've brought them back. Ohh, they're back all

right!" Mrs. Appleplum clapped her hands together and nearly bounced up and down. "Shake this!" she said, handing Fern a gardening book.

Fern was scared. She held the book very gently.

"It's okay," Mrs. Appleplum told her. "It's fine. Shake it!"

And so Fern did, gently at first. Nothing.

"Harder now!" Mrs. Appleplum told her.

Fern shook it harder. And there on her bed plopped a small pile of pansies, dirty roots and all. The book was suddenly lighter, and Fern felt light-headed. She stared at the flowers, then at Mrs. Appleplum, then back at the flowers with their scrawny roots and fine spray of dirt on the bare mattress. She couldn't help remembering the crickets that had hopped out of the picture book when she was four years old. She'd dismissed it, but it was true. It had happened!

"Oh, my!" Mrs. Appleplum hooted.

The Book of Presidents was the next one that Mrs. Appleplum found in the mess. She grabbed it and shoved it at Fern. "This one! This one, too!"

Fern took the book in her hands. It was a very large book. "But, but . . . anything could come out!" Fern said.

"The Civil War could come out!" the Bone blurted.

This made the Miser smile in a twisted way. "Shake it," he said.

161

"Just shake it lightly," Mrs. Appleplum instructed.

And so Fern did. A big black top hat popped out. Fern gasped. "Do you think it's Abraham Lincoln's?"

"Could be! Could be!" Mrs. Appleplum squealed.

"What a mildly interesting little talent," the Miser said. "What a nice little party trick."

The Bone stared at the hat with his mouth wide open, and a grin spread across his face.

Mrs. Appleplum picked up a book off the floor, right in front of her feet. *The Wizard of Oz?* Maybe this is the book that you shook!"

"It's possible," Fern said.

"Well, I'd say we were quite lucky. It could have been worse. It could have been those flying monkeys."

"Well, everyone seems to have escaped without injury," the Miser said. "How lucky indeed!" And he turned and left the messy room.

Mrs. Appleplum got right up close to Fern's face, so close that her eyes were gigantic, two moons! "Oh, dear, you've made me so happy. So very happy." She gave Fern a peck on the cheek. Fern was surprised. She touched the spot of the kiss with her fingers as if to make it stay right there. Then Mrs. Appleplum held up a warning finger. "Just don't pick up any books about that blasted mouse on his motorcycle! He's trouble, I tell you. A menace! And no pirates, please. They're so surly." She started shuffling out the door, down the hall, talking more to herself than to Fern. "And those science books on dinosaurs, no, no, no. Can't have that! Oh, my! Oh, my." She was singing now, joyfully, "It's all coming back! It's all coming back!"

GOLDFISH

"A WONDERFUL GIFT," THE BONE SAID ONCE Mrs. Appleplum was gone. "A truly wonderful gift!" The Bone walked up to Fern, and she wondered if he'd hug her, if he'd give her a peck on the cheek as Mrs. Appleplum had. He looked like he might, but then he shook his head as if reminding himself that he wasn't the type. He started picking up books.

Fern was a little disappointed, but she was too busy to dwell on it, thinking back now, her mind reeling. Had the spider been Fern's imagination? She had a great imagination, you know, but wasn't the spider trying to get at the Bone? Wasn't it the Miser transformed?

Fern explained how the Miser said he had killed a

spider earlier, in his room, and then she saw this spider. "It was coming after you!"

"It was the Miser's doing, that's the truth," said the Bone.

"But, but . . . how? How could he have turned back into himself so quickly after having been a spider that was blown out the window? He was standing right there so calmly."

"He hypnotized you, Fern, just ever so slightly. It's called the power of suggestion. He suggested, very clearly, that you might see a poisonous spider tonight and that it might bite. He has a certain way with his voice, a singsong, that can make you believe something more easily."

"Oh," Fern said. She felt a little foolish. She didn't like the idea that the Miser had gotten one over on her. She didn't like to be tricked. But then she remembered that she knew something the Miser didn't. The diary! "My mother used to keep a diary, when she was a little girl my age! If we find that, then it might lead us to *The Art of Being Anybody*!"

"Well," the Bone said, "even if the diary would lead us to *The Art of Being Anybody*, it's still just another book, another needle in this haystack." He smoothed Fern's windblown hair. "I think we should try to be safe, most of all. I'd die if anything, if anything ever . . ." Fern stood still, hoping he'd finish his sentence if she held on to the moment as best she could. She thought back to the spider hanging on its silver thread over the Bone, and how it had made her panic with fear that something might hurt him. But the Bone turned away from Fern, found the lamp shade on the floor and put it back on the light.

The Bone and Fern untangled the covers on top of the dresser and started clearing the books off their mattresses. Luckily, the tornado had taken a lot of books with it, and the spider, too, although it probably hadn't really existed. Fern began at the bottom of the bed and worked her way up. She found her pillow across the room and was about to put it back at the head of her bed, but there was one more book to be found. This one was very small, leather bound. It had a small golden lock. It was in the exact spot where Mrs. Appleplum had been standing. Had she been standing on it in her orthopedic shoes?

"Look," Fern said, "it's a diary. Do you think it could be . . . ?"

The Bone stopped and turned. "But I went through every book in this room. Each and every one, and I never saw that. I know I didn't," he said.

"It must have been hidden in some way. The tornado must have knocked it loose!" Fern said.

The lock would need a tiny key, and Fern, it just so happened, had one. She sat down on the bed and lifted the necklace from her neck. She untied the string. She fit the key into the lock. It turned and the latch fell open.

Fern was feeling completely magical now. She held the diary close to her heart. She wasn't ready to open it. Not yet. She looked at the painting on the wall. She stood up and walked to it. She remembered the painting in the parlor of a bowl, the kind usually filled with fruit, but it looked like the fruit had been taken away, and the bowl had been refilled with books. Was it possible to reach into a painting? Was it possible to reach into a painting and pull fruit out of the bowl?

The Bone watched quietly as Fern closed her eyes. She wished that something would happen, something unexpected. She lifted her hand to the painting. She inched her hand closer and closer until she felt something give, and then she gently glided her hand inside of it.

She touched a lily first.

"What's it like, Fern?" the Bone asked.

Fern kept her eyes shut tight, afraid that if she opened them it would all disappear. "The petals are soft, velvety soft," she said. And they were. She rubbed them with her fingertips, the way someone would to test a fine silk. She thought, *Things aren't always what they seem, are they? No, no they aren't.*

Fern squeezed her eyes shut even tighter. She felt her way gently along an outline of wet rocks and then reached into the pond. It was wet and cool and the goldfish swirled around her hand so closely they brushed her with their fins. She opened her eyes, slowly, slowly.

The Bone was transfixed, amazed. "It's a beautiful thing!" he said.

There she was, Fern Drudger, up to her elbow in a painting, rings rippling out across the small pond, in the middle of a messy room—a tangle of bed linens and a thousand books, curtains, shoes, pansies, a top hat, her three hateful barrettes lying on the floor—and do you know what she was thinking? She was thinking a thought that only she could think with half her arm inside of a painting after a tornado. She was thinking that this was what home must feel like, this or something very close to it.

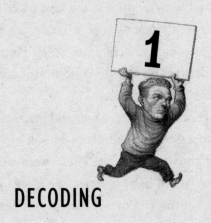

DECODING

HOPEFULLY YOU WERE PAYING ATTENTION IN Part 2, Chapter One. That's where I reported that the Bone told Fern that even Eliza's grocery lists were in some kind of code. Remember? And that meant, of course, her diary was, too. There was only one word that wasn't in code in the diary, and that was Eliza's name, written in curlicue letters on the first page. The rest was a mess of lines, squiggles, and some numbers. At first, Fern spent her evenings trying to decode the diary. She'd had no luck. Then she decided to use her fledgling powers to try to shake the diary, in hopes that—you guessed it—*The Art of Being Anybody* would slip out. This hadn't produced results either, but she was hopeful.

Her days were spent under Mrs. Appleplum's wing, out of doors, which is the best place to shake a book if you aren't exactly sure what's going to come out. Mrs. Appleplum was trying to teach Fern—well, Ida—how to shake a book with concentration so she could better control the outcome.

Fern was getting better and better. She'd wanted white dinner gloves to fall out of a book of manners, and that's exactly what she got. There were still problems—on a book about baby bunnies, she'd only been able to shake out a sprinkling of tiny turd pellets. But all in all, she was improving, and this made Mrs. Appleplum very happy, and making Mrs. Appleplum happy made Fern happy, because deep down Fern wanted Mrs. Appleplum to love Ida Bibb. One day Fern hoped that she would be able to come clean about being Fern, her granddaughter, and she wanted this to come as a pleasant surprise to Mrs. Appleplum.

One afternoon, they toted their books to the cool shade of the giant peach. (I don't have time to describe the peach in detail. I've got to get on with Fern's story. But if you'd like a description of what exactly this peach looked like, you should consult Mr. Roald Dahl's book on the subject. It's quite good.) From this spot, Fern could hear the hobbits' hushed, polite chatter in the brambly front yard—"Do, please." "After you." "Most kind." "Thank you." And twice she thought she saw a mouse skittering through the grass, but on second look, she saw it was the fairy. She was wearing a small gray dress. It was the same dress Mrs. Appleplum had been sewing the night Fern read her the three books. (And how had that come about exactly? Fern didn't know.) Once she thought she caught the fairy shaking her fist in Fern's general direction, which was unusual because one usually thinks of fairies traipsing around maypoles or playing the lute.

Mrs. Appleplum was being demanding, but tender. "Try again," she told Fern. "Try harder."

Fern was concentrating. Her tuft of unruly hair was waving in the wind. She'd woken up one morning to glimpse a very small person hauling her barrettes and pansies away in a basket. Fern remembered Mrs. Appleplum telling her to report any thefts, but Fern didn't need the pansies, and she didn't want those old barrettes anyway. She let the little person take them away. Was it a Borrower? It was highly unexpected to wake up and see a miniature person stealing your things, but Fern was starting to expect the unexpected. Once, while taking out Mrs. Appleplum's garbage, she'd seen a snarling rat that stuck his tongue out at her for no apparent reason.

"Were you able to do this when you were younger?" Fern asked.

"I give my gifts away as often as I can," Mrs.

Appleplum said. "I gave this gift to my daughter, who passed away."

Fern had been waiting for a chance to ask a question about her mother. She tried to sound casual. "What was she like?" Fern asked. She wanted to ask if she smelled like lilacs, but that might be suspicious.

"She was loving. She was smart. She was funny, too. She was the kind of person you always wanted to be with. It was like she had a light that shined out from her face, and when she looked at each person, they shined in her spotlight and flowered into their own most wonderful attributes and deepest good intentions. She looked at each person as though they were the best person in the world."

"Oh," Fern said.

"She was a good bit like you, Ida. A good bit."

This made Fern swell with pride, although she felt guilty that Mrs. Appleplum still thought she was Ida Bibb. She wanted desperately to tell her that she wasn't an encyclopedia salesman's daughter, but Mrs. Appleplum's very own granddaughter. She could barely contain the secret. It seemed to burn in her, a horrible lie. She wanted to tell Mrs. Appleplum the truth so that Mrs. Appleplum could take Fern in her arms and hug her tightly. Fern remembered the exact spot on her cheek where Mrs. Appleplum had kissed her the night she'd shaken her first book. Fern thought, *I'm like my mother, my wonderful mother!* She shook a book on pruning fruit trees, and a hundred apples fell out. Beautiful shiny apples as red as hearts.

The daily lessons were good because they distracted Mrs. Appleplum, allowing the Bone time to pretend to look through books in the kitchen or the living room or the hall closet, while really he was trying to decode the diary. You see, Fern and the Bone had to keep looking through books, or the Miser would get suspicious and know they were on a different scent. The Miser also liked the distraction that Fern caused Mrs. Appleplum. It gave him time to look for the book, as well. And it was always possible that the Miser would get to the book first, by random luck.

In the evenings, Fern would also try to help the Bone get better at becoming Mr. Bibb. The Bone had brought his gold pocket watch and his bells. Fern would sway the watch back and forth. She would say, "You are Mr. Bibb. Mr. Bibb. Mr. Bibb." At the end of the series, she'd ring one bell like crazy. How could they ring the bell, you might ask, without alerting the household? Well, Fern had told Mrs. Appleplum that she was try-ing to learn to play the bells. That she was part of a Christmas chorus at school in which she was crucial to "Jingle Bells," and had to keep practicing or she'd get rusty. And they always waited until the Miser had gone out, which he did every night. "For a walk," he claimed as Mr. Haiserblaitherness, but really he was working his way steadily through the books in the barn. Late at night, after Mrs. Appleplum was fast asleep, they'd seen him out there with a small crew of his spies put to work sorting books. The spies drove up in the red van, the gold letters easily readable—HAISERBLAITHERNESS LIGHTS, PLASTICS, AND TOILETRIES. Fern found it suspicious, a company as weirdly made-up sounding as the last name Haiserblaitherness. And who specializes in lights, plastics, and toiletries all at the same time?

After the bell rang, the Bone would open his eyes. He would walk to the mirror. He almost always had a Mr. Bibb nose. Sometimes he had the black hair—no need for slicking it with shoe polish—and more and more often the mustache was real. And, occasionally, he'd find himself drawn to the topic of encyclopedias and the importance of a set in every American home.

After all of this, Fern would turn her attention to the diary. She spent the hours after dinner shaking the book with as much concentration as she possibly could. The Bone would pace. So far, they'd gotten a movie ticket stub, two pieces of toffee, and a hairbrush. "Is this a diary or a pocketbook?" Fern complained.

The Bone couldn't watch. When something new fell out, he'd whisper, "Is it . . . Is it . . . ?" But when Fern told him "No, it isn't," he'd walk to the window. "Don't tell me. I don't want to see."

Fern understood. It was a mix of sweetness and sadness to have her mother's things suddenly fall into her lap. The hairbrush was especially hard to take, because a few strands of her mother's long dark hair were woven through the brush. Fern put all of her mother's things in her bag. But the brush was progress, Fern felt. It seemed like the items were getting bigger, heavier—from movie stub to toffee to hairbrush . . . so a book didn't seem impossible. Sometimes, when she was alone in the room, she would walk over to the painting of the goldfish and slip her hand inside and try to recapture that feeling she'd had the first time she'd done it. She wanted to feel like she was getting closer to feeling like she was home, but each time she did it now—her hand fanning and swirling around the goldfish—she felt dishonest.

She felt guilty. How could she really feel at home if she was pretending to be Ida Bibb? How could she?

One night after about two weeks, an odd thing happened. The Bone was at the window, keeping watch over the Miser, who had a ladder and a flashlight and had disappeared up the ladder into a tunnel he'd dug through the wall of books in the barn. His spies were with him, their small muscular bodies digging, shuffling. They were whistling, which is a stereotype, really. It's what you think little people would do while they're working—like the seven dwarves—and I don't like stereotypes, but, in this case, the spies were, in fact, whistling, so I must include it. And really they have every right to whistle. There's nothing wrong with whistling while you work, for goodness sake. I've done it. In fact, I'm doing it right now while I'm writing this! (And what would my old writing teacher think of that, ha! Could he write and whistle at the same time? I don't think so!) I knew a boy who whistled all of the time, and his mother said, "Stop whistling. What are you gonna be, a professional whistler when you grow up?" He didn't stop. He learned how to hum melody while whistling harmony and was on *The Tonight Show Starring Johnny Carson* many times. This has nothing to do with little people, but it is a good lesson to learn.

Fern was shaking the diary. She was frustrated because nothing had fallen out in a couple of days. It was as if something were stuck. Fern shook hard, as hard as she could. She felt the book's heaviness. It was as heavy as she'd ever felt a book to be. She shook and shook, and then she saw something poking out. Black leather. She grabbed it with both hands. It had a rubber underside.

"What is it?" the Bone asked, unable to look over at Fern.

Fern pulled and she pulled and she pulled some more, until out popped an orthopedic lace-up shoe complete with a foot and thin, knee-high stockings. Mrs. Appleplum's foot!

Fern let out a yelp. Then she heard a scream.

"What in holy heck!" Mrs. Appleplum cried out from the bathroom. "Help me!"

Fern flipped the diary around. She shook and jiggled until the foot disappeared. The Bone ran to the bathroom and knocked loudly on the door. "Are you okay in there?"

Fern closed the diary and ran to join the Bone. Everything was silent a moment. Mrs. Appleplum opened the door and poked her head out. "I just had the strangest sensation that someone was pulling my leg!" She stared at the Bone, then at Fern.

"Really? You mean a prank? Someone is joking with you?" the Bone asked.

"Humph!" said Mrs. Appleplum. "Never you mind."

And she shut the door.

As soon as they were back in the bedroom, the Bone started asking questions. "What happened? What was it?"

Fern shrugged. "I don't really know," she lied. "Weird. You know, I think Mrs. Appleplum is strange. I think you're right about her."

"But, but what was coming out of the book?"

"Nothing," Fern said, lying some more.

"Are you sure?" the Bone asked, sensing the lie.

"I was just angry with it. Frustrated. I should be more careful."

"Well, that's the truth!" said the Bone.

"Maybe I'll try some decoding," Fern said.

"Good idea. I'm going to rest a minute." The Bone lay down on his bed and, without even much thinking about it, he fell fast asleep.

You must be wondering why Fern would lie like that about Mrs. Appleplum's foot miraculously popping out of a book. Fern was being dishonest, and that's not a good thing to be at all. And Fern was having trouble, in general, pretending to be someone other than herself. But sometimes people tell fibs; sometimes people don't divulge everything they know. (It's true. I once told someone that my mother was a famous flamingo dancer, and I was caught because it's "flamenco" dancer not "flamingo," and this was quite embarrassing for me.

And so I swore off telling lies. That's how you know that every word of this book, every single one, is true!)

Fern was lying because her mind was working very, very quickly. If she could shake out her grandmother's orthopedic rubber-sole shoe, bunions and all, she was wondering if she could shake someone else out of the book. She was, in fact, wondering if she could shake her mother out of the book. Why not? It was, after all, her mother's diary. She knew, deep down, that this wasn't a good idea. She knew that the Bone would probably talk her out of such a thing. Fern didn't tell him because she didn't want to be talked out of it. She wanted her mother to slip out of this book, landing dazed, but beautifully so. She wanted to whisper to her mother, "It's me. Fern. I'm your daughter." And for her mother to wrap her arms around her and kiss her.

And so, once the Bone was asleep, she decided she would give the diary one spectacular shake, one enormously huge shake.

The house was quiet now. Mrs. Appleplum was probably already asleep, like the Bone with his loud snores. The Miser was the only one awake, and he was far off working in the barn with a miniature flashlight gripped in his teeth so he could dig with both hands. But Fern didn't feel at ease in the house. Her mother's appearance could be a noisy one.

So Fern slipped out of her bedroom, her mother's diary clamped under her arm. She walked down the stairs, through the parlor, through the kitchen, to a small back door.

The night was warm, but there was a soft breeze. Fern decided that she would need to be somewhere high, so she could jump down with all of her force. She saw the distant peach tree, its one peach swollen as full as the moon. Fern walked to it and shinnied up the trunk in her pajamas. She climbed out on a thick branch and paused a minute.

"You owe me a favor!" a little voice said. "You! Hey, you!"

Fern looked around. "I . . . I . . ."

"You owe me, I say, I say!" And there at the base of the tree was the redheaded fairy in the gray dress Mrs. Appleplum had sewn with one of Fern's pansies clipped to a belt. (Let me say right up

184

front that I'm not comfortable with this fairy. There's something, each time I write about her, that makes me feel a little silly, like this is a silly book, not one to be taken seriously. And, *I* think at least, that this isn't a silly book at all. But I have to be true to the story. That's what my old writing teacher told me, time and again: Be true to the story. Be true to the story. He'd go on and on with that line like he was beating a drum in the Macy's Thanksgiving Day Parade. (I'm not so sure he knew what he was talking about at all!) In any case, I'm going to be true to the story, and, unfortunately, the story has a fairy in it. An angry fairy, the kind of fairy who would put a bumper sticker on her car that said something like, IF YOU CAN READ THIS, YOU'RE TOO CLOSE TO MY CAR. BACK OFF! That is, if fairies had cars, which I don't think they do.)

"You shouldn't be out here, you know," the fairy said. "You should be practicing. There are a lot of us here who are counting on you!"

"Counting on me?"

"Yes, you! Who else!" The fairy was angry. Her face was pinched as if she'd bitten into a bitter prune. "I can't understand how dense you *people* are!"

"Dense!" Fern said. "I'm not so dense that I don't know when someone's stolen something from me. Is that pansy yours? Where, then, are my barrettes?"

The fairy was furious now. "This pansy and those

barrettes were a gift from a friend! How dare you!" And she shook her tiny fist in the air, menacingly. "I could bite you when you least expect it, right on the ankle, and my teeth are sharp." She stormed off, back toward the house.

Fern didn't care about the pansies or the barrettes at all, but she hadn't liked being called dense either. She hadn't been expecting to be confronted like this. But maybe the fairy was right and Fern did owe her something. She had shaken her from the comfortable confines of her book onto the floor, mid-bath, but she didn't understand who else was counting on her. And counting on her for what, exactly?

Fern felt nervous. She opened the diary and noticed that her hands were trembling. But she had to go through with it. She had to. If her mother came out of the book, oh, how she would thank Fern. *My angel! You saved me! You've brought me back!*

Fern opened the book as wide as she possibly, possibly could. She drew the diary up over her head with one hand, and swung the diary down as hard as she could while jumping from the branch. Her hair lifted up over her head. Her pajamas billowed like a parachute. The night air was cool on her skin, and the diary was heavy, so heavy that Fern hit the ground hard, bruising her knees and the heels of her hands. The diary had come loose from her grip, but Fern wasn't thinking about that now. At the same moment Fern had fallen, there had been another, louder thump. Fern's eyes were closed, but she knew something was before her, something alive, breathing. She whispered, "Oh, please, oh, please." And when she opened her eyes she was blinded by a bright, bright light. There was an angry voice. "What is this? What have you done, Miss BIBB?" A dark figure rose from the roots of the tree. It was the Miser. He said the word "Bibb" like an accusation. "How on earth did I get here! I was just in the barn, and now I'm here. How . . . magical!" He lowered his voice. "You are in trouble, Miss Bibb. Deep, deep trouble!"

"Actually, I can clear all of this up. I can clear it right up!" Fern started rambling fast. This time she felt skilled at it and used the chatter, which might have once stayed stored in her head, to hold the Miser's attention. It worked for a little while. . . . "I'm very good at clearing things up. In fact, if there were awards for clearing things up, then I would have a ton of awards and tro-phies and medals. That's how good I am at it! And if you ask me, I think there should be awards for things like the ability to clear things up. It would be nice if things were, in general, clearer. In my opinion . . ." but then the Miser's interest started to wander. His flashlight glanced away from Fern's face to the diary on the ground.

"What, oh, what have we here? Is this a diary? Have

you shaken me through a diary? Who's been writing about me?" He picked up the book and opened to the front page.

"Don't," Fern said.

But it was too late. "Eliza? My Eliza?" the Miser said. His voice became soft. His shoulders curled toward the book. He was astonished, suddenly wide-eyed with love. The Miser said, "Oh, how she loved me! She loved me!" And in a weird trancelike state, he held on to his flashlight and the diary, turned and seemed to nearly float across the yard to the back door.

Fern followed him, although he paid her no attention. "I need that diary," she said. "Excuse me, but it's quite important that I have that diary!"

The Miser opened the screen door and it slammed before Fern had the chance to catch it. Just as she put her hand on the small metal handle, she heard Mrs. Appleplum's voice. Fern pressed her back to the side of the house and froze.

"What's this? Mr. Haiserblaitherness! What are you doing up and about? Are you okay? What's that glaze to your eyes? Have you been sleepwalking?"

"Yes!" Fern said, now tripping in the door. "He has been sleepwalking! I saw him from my window and I followed him around to the back of the house."

The Miser snapped to. He glanced at Fern and then at Mrs. Appleplum and around the kitchen. "What? I haven't been sleepwalking! That little girl, she, she—"

"Hush now," Mrs. Appleplum said.

"No, you don't understand!"

"You've had a bad dream, dear," Mrs. Appleplum said reassuringly. "You know it's quite dangerous to sleepwalk. Come. Come. Take my hand."

The Miser shrank a bit, glowering at Fern over his shoulder. He took Mrs. Appleplum's hand with grave embarrassment. Mrs. Appleplum wasn't someone you could say no to. They filed through the kitchen maze, through the parlor.

"Here, I'll hold this stuff for you," Fern offered, taking ahold of the diary and the flashlight.

"No," the Miser said, snatching them back. "Don't you dare!"

"No, no, now, Mr. Haiserblaitherness! Don't raise your voice like that! You need to let go of these things. Ida is being courteous, and we have to encourage that in children or we'll raise a generation with no manners at all!"

The Miser sighed deeply. Mrs. Appleplum took the diary and flashlight and handed them to Fern. "Thank you, Ida," Mrs. Appleplum said.

Fern grabbed on to the diary and the flashlight, feeling very relieved.

The Bone met them at the bottom of the stairs. "I heard a commotion. Isss everything all right?"

Mrs. Appleplum explained, "Mr. Haiserblaitherness has been sleepwalking. Will you two, Ida and Mr. Bibb, do me a favor and tie him down for the night? He could get hurt if he sleepwalks again!"

"No, no," the Miser said. "Not necessary! I'm fine!"

"No problem," said the Bone. "We don't mind! We'd be happy to tie Mr. Haissserblaithernesss down for the night!"

"See what good friends you've made? They don't mind helping you out in your time of need, Mr. Haiserblaitherness, not one bit! Stay here while I get some rope!"

SSSSSSSSSSS!

MRS. APPLEPLUM WENT DOWNSTAIRS TO GET ROPE from a utility closet next to the kitchen. It stored mostly books, of course, but there were also a few light bulbs, tulip bulbs, a screwdriver—the general utilities. She left Fern and the Bone and the Miser in the hallway together, where the Miser was unlocking his bedroom door.

"This isn't necessary!" the Miser said.

"Isn't it, Mr. Haiserblaitherness?" Fern asked.

"No, it isn't and you know it!"

The Bone said calmly, "Do you want to tell Mrss. Appleplum that you AREN'T Mr. Haissserblaithernesss, but you are, in fact, the Missser!"

Fern held on tightly to the diary. Her eyes darted between the two men. The Bone looked like Mr. Bibb, but tough. His chin jutted out defiantly.

Although Fern couldn't see the Miser's eyes beneath his enormous saggy eyebrows, she knew that he was glaring at the Bone, his cheeks flushed a deep red. "I could blow your cover too, you know that!"

"I would blow your cover firsst!" the Bone countered.

"And then we'd all be thrown out of this house," Fern whispered. "Is that a good idea?"

Just then, Mrs. Appleplum was climbing the stairs with her brittle bones. "I've got it!" she sang out in a rippling voice. "Here." She handed the rope to the Bone. "Now," she said, sighing. "I'm going to bed. Best of luck! I'll be up early in the morning to untie you." She gave the Miser a pat-pat on his shoulder.

And Mrs. Appleplum walked off to her bedroom at the end of the hall.

The Miser opened his bedroom door and rushed to a small writing table covered with a pile of what looked to be hand-scrawled notes on white sheets of paper. He stuffed them into his pockets. It was a small, hot room, also piled high with books. There was one dark window open just a crack. There was a black trunk, closed, and a large empty sack on the floor. Fern remembered that when they had first arrived, Mrs. Appleplum told them about another guest who had shown up with a trunk and a large unusual sack, stuffed tight. Fern wondered what had been in it.

"Let's get this over with," the Miser said bitterly, lying down on his narrow bed.

The Bone and Fern started to secure the ropes as best they could, but Fern wasn't so sure that it mattered. Couldn't he easily get out of ropes? He'd already turned into a bull, for goodness sake!

"I've still got my men working. My little army is shoveling through books in the barn at this very moment. And these ropes are a formality, you know," the Miser said. "I've gotten to be quite a good Anybody, Bone. I've gotten better at transforming than you'd have ever imagined. You realize that your daughter here shook me from a book. Not just any book. She shook me from Eliza's diary." The Bone glanced sharply at Fern, who didn't look at him but kept her head down, fiddling with the ropes. "Eliza loved me, Bone. She was writing about me. She was writing that she loved me! Think about it, Bone. Think!"

The Bone reared. He turned away from the Miser, but Fern kept maneuvering around with the ropes, tying this way and that. A breeze kicked up from the window, and there was a rustling noise under the bed. She wondered if anyone else had heard it. She didn't think so. The room was charged with angry tension between the Miser and the Bone.

The Miser kept at it. "And look at you! Mr. Bibb, ha! You can't even pull off a successful encyclopedia salesman. Is it slipping? That fake mustache of yours?"

"No!" the Bone said. "It'sss real!"

"Oh, and that lisp is real too? I can't believe you were once my teacher!"

Fern gave the ropes an extra angry yank and knotted them on a leg of the bed, which gave her the opportunity to peek underneath. There she saw a remarkable sight. A white fluttering sea of paper. Now she knew what had been in the stuffed sack. Envelopes. Some thin, some fat, but envelopes, envelopes, envelopes, addressed and stamped. Why didn't he just leave them in the sack? Fern wondered. Why did he put them under the bed? Was he the type who needed to unpack to feel settled—the Drudgers always unpacked their suitcases and folded their clothes in hotel bureaus, as a rule—or was it that, for some reason, he liked to go through the envelopes, sorting them? What was in those envelopes? Was it some evil that comforted him? The wind kicked up again and they rustled like birds.

The Miser didn't seem aware of Fern at all. "You're worthless now, Bone, and you were worthless then." The Bone was turned toward the door, his back bristling. He couldn't look at the Miser. "How could she have ever truly loved you, Bone. I'll find that book first. I'm smarter than you. Think about it! I'll find the book first. . . . Think about it! Think about it!" The Miser's voice was changing now. Fern recognized the singsong of hypnosis. Fern was scared suddenly. Was the Miser trying to hypnotize the Bone? She thought of grabbing a few envelopes, not many, just a few, but she couldn't. She didn't have pockets. She was holding the diary. How would she hide the envelopes? She wanted to know what was inside of them, but she didn't have time. She needed to get the Bone away from that voice!

She stood up. "Let's go!"

"Think about it, think about it, think, think. I'm close to finding that book. I'm so close. You'll never beat me to it. Think about it," the Miser was saying.

"Stop it!" Fern said to the Miser. "Stop! It won't work." She grabbed her father's arm, opened the door and shoved the Bone into the hallway.

"Sssstop," the Miser said. Fern wasn't sure if he was mocking her or the Bone or both of them. The Miser was shaking now, his whole body trembling under the ropes. "Sssstop. Sssssss," he said. He gave one violent shake and his body writhed into the shape of a large gray snake, its scales glinting in the lamplight. The snake hissed at Fern as it started slipping from the ropes.

Fern grabbed the Miser's key off his small desk, jumped out the door. She slammed it, and locked the room up tight.

195

Fern and the Bone walked quickly down the hallway. They stepped into their bedroom and shut the door. The Bone looked rattled, worn-out, like a wind-beaten kite.

"Are you okay?" Fern asked. She felt giddy.

"What if he *is* close, Fern? His spies are digging right now!" the Bone said, glancing out the window toward the barn. "What if he finds *The Art of Being Anybody* first?"

"Are you sure you're okay? He didn't hypnotize you, did he?"

"Of course not! I know his tricks! I was humming a song in my head. I was blocking him out with it."

Fern knew the song he'd been humming: *Sweet, sweet, my sweet darling angel, where have you gone, where have you gone?* It seemed to always be on his mind. "You know what was in that sack of his? Letters! That's what he does in there when he isn't looking for books. He's writing letters!" Fern said.

"He used to write letters when he was a good Anybody. He used to write the loveliest letters . . . invitations, apologies. He used to write love letters to your mother, and they made her cry, because she didn't love him back, but they were so beautiful. Can you imagine what kind of letters he's writing now? Hate mail. Blackmail. Who knows! But I can tell you this, I'm going to stay up late tonight and decode this diary. I'm sure Eliza would have confided where she hid that book. I'm sure she would!"

"I hope so," Fern said, sitting down on her bed. "I hope there are some clues. We have no clues!"

The Bone sat down next her. "Fern," he said, "I wanted. . . ," but then he trailed off.

"What?" Fern asked.

"I wanted to tell you that I know."

"What?"

"I know why you shook the diary so hard." He paused. "It doesn't work that way." He shook his head. His eyes were misty again, and Fern wondered if he would ever really cry. "She can't come back. She was buried in a cemetery. There's a tombstone with her name on it. She can't come out of a book. Your mother, she's gone."

"Oh," Fern said. She felt like crying, but she didn't either. She kind of knew that it wouldn't work. It had been a long shot. She said, "I just thought . . ."

"I know," the Bone said. "I know what you thought." He squeezed her shoulder, and then they both fell quiet, so quiet that the only thing they could hear was the Miser, hissing in his locked room down the hall.

3

THE UPRISING

"FINISH YOUR BREAKFAST QUICKLY, DEAR! Quickly! I knew this day would come," Mrs. Appleplum was chirping in the kitchen. "Oh, my," she said. "I just knew it. Hurry, hurry!"

Fern was eating toast with marmalade, which reminded her of a bear who lived in England named Paddington, a British bear whom she used to read about when she was a bit younger. She'd actually planned on canceling her lesson with Mrs. Appleplum today. She wanted to go back upstairs to relieve the Bone, who'd been trying to decode the diary all night while she slept. She wanted to switch places with him. He looked awful, bleary-eyed and bedraggled. "What is

199

it?" Fern asked. "Is it Mr. Haiserblaitherness? Has he done something?"

"Done something?" Mrs. Appleplum looked at her, perplexed. "No, I don't think so. Do you think he's broken something in his room? He'll have to pay for that, you know."

"No, I was just asking . . ."

"Mr. Haiserblaitherness is fine, as far as I know. I untied him this morning. He looked well-rested. But I do wonder if your father's lisp isn't contagious, because Mr. Haiserblaitherness sure had a strange *s* in his words."

"Well, I've never caught the lisp," Fern said, although she knew very well why Mr. Haiserblaitherness was still a bit hissy. She'd been thinking about him this morning. Those envelopes were on her mind. What was he writing? Why did he keep them even after addressing and stamping them? Why didn't he just mail them?

Mrs. Appleplum went on, "In any case, the point is— are you done eating?"

Fern nodded.

"The point is— Come on. Come on." She held on to Fern's arm and walked her briskly to the back door. "We have a problem."

Fern opened the screen door and stared at the backyard. Straight ahead beside the giant peach tree was a line of creatures. She recognized some—furry-footed hobbits and the redheaded fairy still wearing the pansy, now slightly wilted, clipped to her belt. There was also a scowling rat, perhaps the same one who'd stuck his tongue out at her, and two rabbits—one nervous older rabbit and the other younger, more casual, almost cool, if a rabbit can be cool. Fern recognized them from the front yard, where she'd once seen them chatting together. And there was one squirrel who was—squirrelly.

(Here, let me interrupt, if you'd be so kind, to say . . . if you think I had trouble writing about the fairy, you can imagine that I'm going to struggle with the hobbits, and, well, the talking animals will be my downfall. I don't like talking animals, as a rule. Not that I would be rude to a talking animal if I came across one. I wouldn't, of course! But luckily I've never had that kind of awkward encounter. I suppose Aesop started the trend—well, there was that serpent who talked to Eve in the garden—but why did the trend have to persist? Generation after generation with their talking animals! It's ridiculous. I wish I didn't have to be a party to it. And yet, I'm handcuffed to the story here. And, sorry to say, in this story there are some talking animals. It's not my fault. It's the fault of the people who wrote the other books in the first place. I guess this is what I'm saying: if you are deeply offended by talking animals, I completely understand.

Fern, unlike me, was fine with talking animals. Some people are. And so . . .)

"What do they want?" Fern asked.

"They want you!"

"Why me?" Fern asked.

"They need help, Ida. And you're the only one who can help them."

Fern was worried. She remembered the mean fairy from the night before. She was a little afraid of her. "How?"

Mrs. Appleplum steered her toward them. "Smile," she said. "It'll make them more at ease."

Fern smiled. The line of creatures shuffled and tittered anxiously.

"How can I help them?" Fern asked.

"The books," Mrs. Appleplum said through her teeth, smiling. "The books."

The fairy started first. "I've organized this uprising! There are things we need! And some of us want to go back! She's got to help us. It's not our fault we're here!"

"Now, now, let's remain civilized," said the nervous rabbit in a genteel

British accent. "Don't make her angry." Fern could see that he was fiddling with a gold watch on a chain, somewhat like the one the Bone used for hypnosis, but this one was much, much smaller.

The rat paced. "Just get on with it!"

The squirrel blinked and flicked its tail.

The hobbits looked skittish and a little sheepish. One said, "We only want what's simple. We have but simple needs. And only if it isn't any trouble. We don't want to trouble you."

"Wait, just wait," Fern said. "Are you all angry because you're not in your books?"

The fairy said, "I want to go back!" But the others shook their heads. The nervous rabbit raised his hand. "I may like to go back, perhaps." But the younger rabbit nudged him in the ribs, and said to Fern, "No, he don't."

They decided to go one at a time. The hobbits, it turned out, much preferred living here in Mrs. Appleplum's front yard. It was safer and quieter than the book they'd come from, and they could enjoy their routines, their small comforts. It was just that they missed some of their favorite ale and tea and pipe weed.

Mrs. Appleplum had already compiled the books Fern would need. *The Hobbit* was the first book in the pile. Fern concentrated and shook, and sure enough she got a nice barrel of ale and a few canisters of tea. "Are you sure you need the pipe weed? Is it really good for you?" she asked.

They shuffled their furry feet. "Not especially," one admitted with a little cough.

"This is fine," another said. "Thank you so very much. We aren't worthy of this much goodness." And another, "How can we repay you? We must repay you! Thank you so kindly!"

The chubby hobbits started rolling their barrel to their underground homes in the front yard. They were very spirited. "We should taste it, don't you think?"

"At this hour of the day?"

"We shouldn't drink it. We should simply taste it to see if it's made it through well enough."

"I suppose we could." And the other nodded, and soon they'd gotten cups and were sipping the ale, tasting and tasting to make sure it hadn't soured.

The young rabbit introduced himself as Peter and he was wearing his blue jacket, but it was a mess—grass-stained elbows, the brass buttons all popped loose. "He wants to get rid of his watch," Peter told Fern, pointing with a jerk of his head to the older rabbit. "He wants it to go back in the book."

"You see," said the older rabbit. "I'm always afraid I'm late, terribly late, for something quite important. And Peter has really taught me that I must calm myself and have adventures."

"Do you agree with him?" Fern asked.

"I do, but I'm frightened."

"Well, the problem is that I can't put things back in books. I can only get them out."

The redheaded fairy erupted. "Well, what good are you then?" And she started to stomp off.

But then Mrs. Appleplum whispered, "Actually, you *can* put things back. I just haven't shown you how to yet. It's quite easy." Fern remembered then that when Mrs. Appleplum's foot had started to come out of the book, she did jiggle it back in as fast as she could.

"Wait! Wait!" Fern yelled to the fairy. "I can try!"

So the redheaded fairy slouched back to the group.

"Let me start with the gold watch," Fern said.

The old rabbit handed Fern the watch hesitantly.

"Are you sure?"

"He's sure," Peter said.

Mrs. Appleplum placed the gold watch on top of the open pages of *Alice's Adventures in Wonderland*. "Concentrate," she said. "Jiggle softly." And sure enough, like sifting sand, the gold watch disappeared into the book.

"Did it work? Did it work?" the fairy asked.

"Yes, yes, it did," announced Mrs. Appleplum.

"What do you want?" Fern asked the rat.

"My name is Templeton."

"Oh, I know you!" Fern said. "I'm named. . . ," but she stopped herself just in time. She didn't want to bring up the girl named Fern in *Charlotte's Web*, which Mrs. Appleplum had on top of the pile now. She corrected herself and said, "I'm named Ida Bibb."

"Great. Fine. I'd rather not say it to the whole group, okay?"

"Okay," Fern said, and she bent down so he could whisper.

"I miss, you know, folks in the book."

"You mean Wilbur?"

"Shhh." His eyes darted around. "Well, maybe."

"Do you want to go back?"

"Keep it down, would you?" Templeton said, then he added loudly, "It's just that they need me in that darn book! I'm very important. Everything will fall apart without me!"

"Okay, okay." Fern let Templeton climb up on the book. She jiggled and he started to sink in. He gave a sharp nod for a good-bye. But as soon as he was gone, his rump reappeared. He was pushed back out. "Let me in!" Fern could hear him shouting. "Come on! Let me back in!" Finally, after a bit of a struggle, he was securely in the book. Fern shut it quickly.

That left the fairy and the squirrel. The fairy said, "I want to go back. You see, I love it there. It's a wonderful place."

"Let's try," Fern said.

The fairy climbed up onto the opened pages of *The Complete Guide to Fairies*. "Wait," she said, handing Fern the barrettes and starting to unclip the pansy. "Here, these are yours. The Borrowers gave them to me."

"You can keep them," Fern told her. "They were never really me, if you know what I mean."

"Thank you," the fairy said. "If this works, if you pull this off, you can shake this book anytime and you'll have a whole army of fairies to help you. That's a promise."

"Thanks," Fern said, and she concentrated very hard. (She was still afraid of a nasty ankle bite.) She jiggled, and the fairy disappeared.

"One left," Mrs. Appleplum said. "Now what book are you from?" she asked the squirrel.

The squirrel was glancing around at the house and

up the tree and at the hobbits who, quite unlike themselves, had gotten so joyously carried away, they were singing a pub song about a woman named Adeline. One belched and excused himself profusely, and then another farted, terribly embarrassed. Fern could smell the cheesy air from where she stood downwind.

"What do you want?" Fern asked the squirrel. "Do you want something?"

But the squirrel didn't really want anything. As it turned out, he was just a regular squirrel. And thank goodness for that! I really needed just a regular squirrel! He blinked his eyes and dashed off.

WILD DRUDGERS
ON TAMED HEDGE ROAD

JUST THEN, THE BONE STUCK HIS HEAD OUT THE back door.

"Ida! Meet me at the car! We've got to head out! We've got a . . . a . . . an errand to run!" He looked at Mrs. Appleplum. "Encsssyclopediasss! Jusst a quick jaunt."

Mrs. Appleplum looked at Fern. "Thank you for helping. You're very good, you know."

"Thanks," said Fern, and then she nearly reached out and grabbed Mrs. Appleplum. She could feel her arms almost rise up and hug her. Fern remembered the kiss Mrs. Appleplum had planted on her cheek. Fern wanted to hug her, but would Mrs. Appleplum hug her back? Fern couldn't be sure, and so she didn't. She resisted. Instead, she ran off, bounding past the tipsy hobbits, who thanked her again with a small chorus of proper cheer, and around the house into the Bone's wheezing car.

The Bone drove the wobbly car down the long driveway, the diary jostling on the seat between them.

"Where are we going?" Fern asked.

"Howard!" the Bone said. "Howard is the key. It struck me, Fern. This diary is a pattern. And patterns can be mathematic equations. The diary has words and numbers like algebra. Howard will be able to crack this code, I tell you."

Howard! Of course, why hadn't Fern thought of him? Howard was at the Drudgers'. "Are you taking me back to Tamed Hedge Road?"

The Bone nodded. "Where else?"

What would she think of her house now that she'd been through so very much? She went through the dates in her head. Math camp would be over with. That was good. And vacation at Lost Lake wouldn't start for a while yet. Would the Drudgers have missed her? Had she missed them?

While they drove, Fern told the Bone about the hobbits, the rabbits, Templeton and the squirrel. "Do you ever think we'll need an army of fairies?"

"You never can tell."

"I almost hugged Mrs. Appleplum," Fern said.

"You didn't tell her that you're her granddaughter, did you?"

"No," Fern said. "Of course not." What she didn't say was that she really wanted to, that she was dying to tell her.

"Good," the Bone said. "Keep your eyes peeled for butterflies. I've asked the Great Realdo to help us out. And, well, that's the form he likes to take with me."

Fern kept watch. They passed an old gas station. It was boarded up, but through its dusty windows, Fern could see that it was packed with old stuff—furniture and dusty junk. The old pumps looked familiar, and Fern remembered the background of the photograph of her mother, swaying, maybe dancing.

They drove on until Fern knew the streets, the familiar turns. There was a certain well-worn comfort. She closed her eyes as the car got closer to Tamed Hedge Road. There was no denying the gravitational pull toward her old house. The pause at the stop sign. The dip in the intersection. The clunk of the manhole cover. The Bone bumped the car over the curb and into the driveway. Her body knew its way there so well. Had this been home all along and she just hadn't been able to recognize it? Maybe! Wouldn't that be a simple fix. Fern opened her eyes, and there they were . . . the cream house with cream shutters on Tamed Hedge Road. Fern felt a familiar tightening in her chest. She narrowed her eyes; it was an instinct. She patted down the front fluff of her wild hair. *No,* Fern thought, *this isn't home. This is the Drudgers' home, not mine.*

Now, I'm sure you haven't been thinking too much about Howard's vacation with the Drudgers, but I can tell you it's been an unusual one. First of all, no matter how happily ordinary Howard is, no matter how much he admired and craved the Drudgers' dullness, he was brought up by the Bone. And there's no avoiding the fact that the Bone had influenced him. The Bone had made him a little adventurous . . . just a little tiny bit. So this is what happened: Howard became very good friends with Milton Beige, the chubby beige boy with the ball-tipped nose whom Fern was supposed to marry one day. While doing math problems for fun, Howard told Milton a secret. It slipped out. Hypnosis. Milton goaded Howard into proving it. "I don't believe you!" he said. So Howard decided to make it clear. Howard wasn't a great hypnotist. Keep that in mind. He was taught by the Bone, who was in a fragile state and not very confident in his own skills. So . . .

It only took a second for Fern to notice that something was wrong at the Drudger household. The grass was much too long. The boxy front hedge had a few wild branches shooting up from it. There was grass growing in the sidewalk cracks, and the racket of crickets, which she'd never heard before from her yard, was noisy.

Fern jumped out of the car. She raced to the front door.

"What is it, Fern? What's wrong?" the Bone asked. To his untrained eye, things seemed just fine.

"It's all wrong!" Fern told him.

She twisted the doorknob, but it was locked. She pounded on the door and buzzed the bell, one long buzz. Then she stopped and listened. She heard weird noises, screeching? Did she hear screeching?

"Who is it?" asked a voice that Fern didn't recognize.

"It's me. Ida. No, Fern, Fern . . . " She nearly said Fern Drudger, but she then thought, *No, Bone*. By this point, Fern didn't know what to say. "Just let me in!" she said. "This is my house!"

"Oh. Well, this is Milton Beige, and I'm unable to open the door at this moment. I . . . I just can't right now. Why don't you come back later?"

"Open up, Milton!" Fern said.

The Bone was standing next to her now. "Open the door. I'm here, too. Tell Howard that it's the Bone."

The door unlocked, and Milton's round nose and big beige cheeks appeared. "Come in, quick," he said.

Howard, his face flushed, was standing behind

Milton. "Hello," he said with a sigh.

Fern and the Bone were hustled inside. The house was a wreck. The ceiling light in the hall entranceway was gone. In its place was a splotch of broken plaster and a handful of wires.

"We can explain," said Milton, his voice high with nerves. "See, we got a little bored—"

"I made a mistake," Howard said. "It's all my fault."

"See, I didn't know it until I met Howard, but I've been bored all my life!" Milton broke in. "But, see . . ."

"No," Fern said. "I don't see! What happened?" Frustrated, she pushed past Howard and Milton and ran from room to room. The closet doors were thrown open and coats and scarves were strewn everywhere. Mr. Drudger's work umbrella was popped open and hanging from the ceiling fan slowly revolving in the kitchen. There were muddy footprints, small like a dog's footprints, all over the beige carpeting. Banana peels splayed on the coffee table. The Drudgers' painting of their living room in their living room was completely crooked. And still there were screechy noises coming from upstairs. And padding. And thumping.

"What's happened here, Howard?" the Bone asked.

"I made a mistake. I wanted to impress Milton. I wanted to prove I could do it. And Milton had a gold watch from his grandfather. I showed it to the Drudgers. I rocked it back and forth and their eyes latched on so easily. I wanted them to be fun! I wanted them to have fun!"

Milton broke in, "Honestly, sir, for all the bad stuff that's happened here, I can honestly say that I *have* had fun. And the Drudgers, sir, *are* more fun."

Fern was charging up the stairs now. She followed the noises until she came to her parents' bedroom. The door was closed. She paused, and Howard charged to the door, blocking it with his body. "Look, Fern, they were so dull I had to do something. I had to at least try!"

"Let me see, Howard, for myself," Fern said.

She pushed Howard out of the way and opened the door. And there they were. Mr. and Mrs. Drudger . . . they were still dressed like themselves, khakis, button-downs. But Mrs. Drudger was jumping on the bed and Mr. Drudger was hanging on the doorknob of the closet. They were both squat and waddling, their chins out, their lips pursing and unpursing. They were ooh-oohing and hee-heeing. Mrs. Drudger's hair was wild and some-what matted. Mr. Drudger was unshaven.

The Bone said, "Yep, I've seen this kind of thing before. Our system isn't perfect. It has . . ."

"Some kinks!" Fern said. "I'd say it has some kinks!"

Milton was standing in the hallway too, breathless from having bounded up the stairs. He wasn't used to such exercise. "Aren't they magnificent creatures?"

"You are a menace," Fern said. "How could you two

do this? It's completely unfair. How long have they been like this, Howard? How long?"

Milton walked into the bedroom. He pulled some grapes out of his pockets, and the Drudgers waddled over to him. They plucked the grapes from his dimpled

hand and popped them into their mouths.

"A week, I guess. I tried to get in touch, but you all weren't home. Have you moved?"

"Just for a little bit," the Bone said.

"And you didn't tell me?" Howard looked hurt.

"We aren't far," the Bone said. "We're trying to get the book. We're getting closer. It's why we're here." The Bone handed Howard the diary. "We found this, but we need it decoded, and I thought if anyone could do it, you could."

Howard eyed the diary. "I can try, I guess," he said.

Fern was still in shock. She was watching Mr. and Mrs. Drudger eat grapes and pick at Milton's hair. "We should try to get them back, shouldn't we?" Fern questioned. But then she really looked at them. They were all cuddled up, talking to each other in a low monkey chatter. They appeared so loving now, as one sniffed the other's head. "Shouldn't we?"

"I love them like this!" Milton smiled. "Let them be happy a little while longer. Just a little! You don't understand," he said. "This is a beautiful thing, I tell you."

The Bone shrugged.

Howard said, "I've tried. They just won't look at me long enough to really settle into dehypnosis. It's like they know and they don't want to. It'll wear off."

Milton said, "We bought a monkey costume. Howard is going to take Mr. Drudger to the bank and get him to cash some checks. I think folks will think he's being funny, you know, annoyingly in character. But they've got to let him take the money out."

"Sounds like a clever plan. And you know I love clever plans. But are you okay?" the Bone asked Howard. "Really?"

"It is actually kind of fun. I sort of like taking care of them. And, you know, it's good for Milton. Look at him."

Milton was climbing on the bed now, jumping with them. Fern smiled. "Well, I guess it's good for them all, somehow."

Howard opened the diary. "This might take a while," he said. "It might be a tough code to crack."

"You can do it!" Fern said.

"I'll try," Howard said.

He walked them downstairs to the front door.

"Did they get fired from Beige & Beige?" Fern asked.

"No, Milton told me to call in some personal vacation time. You know they had a lot of unused vacation days!"

"I know," Fern said. She wandered away from the Bone and Howard into the living room. She walked to the painting of the living room and moved it so that it hung straight. She could hear the Bone saying "Here's my phone number. Call us as soon as you think you've got it," and Howard saying that he would, as soon as he could.

Howard and the Bone didn't hug. The Bone didn't do that kind of thing. While they shook hands, Fern shut her eyes and slowly lifted her hand to the painting. Then she tried to glide her fingers into the painting, thinking to herself, *No, it isn't possible. It couldn't be. Not here.* Her fingers were stopped. They bounced off the canvas. Then she heard the monkey noises overhead, and she tried again, thinking this time that it *was* possible, that anything was possible, really, that things weren't what they seemed to be. And this time her fingers did slip into the painting. Fern patted the fuzz of the beige carpeting, a replica of the beige carpeting she was standing on at that very moment. Fern was astonished that she'd had this power all along and had never known it. Feeling jittery, she pulled her hand out of the painting and walked quickly back to Howard and the Bone.

"I'm proud of you, son," the Bone said. "You're part my boy, even though you're a Drudger. You know that?"

Just then there was loud screeching from upstairs, the Drudgers howling like monkeys. "There's no denying it," Howard said. "No denying it."

5
THE LIMP

STAY FOCUSED NOW! STAY SHARP! THAT'S MY advice, because things may pick up speed and get a little jostled like those roller coaster boxcars on their tight, loopy tracks, and I don't want you to topple out, or something dreadful like that. I'm doing the best I can, and I can't think of any advice from my old writing instructor that would help me now. He never wrote a book with so much going on. In fact, his books are dry and dusty, big fatty books that sit on library shelves until you check them out just to let them get some air, because you feel sorry for them. I hope the rest of this goes well. I can hear that roller coaster motor chugging and whining and, actually, I don't like roller coasters. Once I got off one and threw up on my shoes.

The Miser has had some time to think. Once he turned himself back into the Miser and especially while he was waiting for Mrs. Appleplum to shuffle in and untie him, he was thinking. He was shaking the blurred vision of love from his head and he was putting things together. He knew Fern had Eliza's diary and that Fern was jiggling things from it. That's how the Miser ended up under the peach tree. And if Eliza had written about *The Art of Being Anybody*—how couldn't she have?—Fern could possibly even shake the book from the diary. So he was nearly convinced that Fern already had *The Art of Being Anybody*, or almost. By the time he was untied and striding out of his room, he had one more question: what was more important to Fern than the book? What?

The old jalopy was acting up, even more than usual. When the Bone and Fern drove in the long driveway and parked, the Bone got out of the car and lifted its rusted hood to look at the engine. Fern went inside the house to tell Mrs. Appleplum that they were expecting a very important phone call, and that they'd want to answer the phone from now on, if that was okay with her.

"Mrs. Appleplum?" Fern called. "Mrs. Appleplum?"

There was no answer. So Fern called out again, but this time she called for Mr. Haiserblaitherness. You see, ever since Fern was in the Miser's room, she was dying to know what he was writing. The letters in those envelopes hadn't gone very far from her mind. Was it part of a dastardly plot of his? The house seemed empty. Maybe this was her chance. She walked up the stairs, calling again and again for Mr. Haiserblaitherness. Still no answer. She called once more, in front of his door, then turned the knob. It opened easily. (She'd taken the key the night before, and he'd had no way of locking it on his way out.)

Fern couldn't help but think there was something alive in the room. The window was open wide now, and the envelopes under the bed were still rustling. Fern moved to the desk. There were envelopes with Mrs. Appleplum's address on them and other letters sitting out. Fern started reading.

Dear Mrs. Appleplum,

I'm sorry I didn't attend breakfast. And apologize for any rudeness last night. I am not myself.

Sincerely,

M.

The next letter read:

Dear Mother,

The wind is warm here. And I miss you terribly. Tell sister

Imogene that I think of her. I often wonder if she married the grocer. I hope Father's back has held up from all of his strongman lifting and that he's stopped eating those nails. It isn't good for his digestion. It's been so many years since I've been in touch. As you know, I haven't been myself.

Love,

M.

There were letters to Imogene, to the grocer, to the Miser's old landlord, an apology for lying—he had, in fact, sealed some small holes in the walls with toothpaste and had left milk in the refrigerator to sour. Fern started opening envelopes under the bed. There were letters to his old piano teacher thanking her for her kindness and apologizing for his lack of diligent practicing, and long weepy epics to his nanny. There were letters to the Bone. They were warm and honest and filled with regret. Fern was shocked. All of the letters ended the same way: *As you know, I haven't been myself.*

Who was the Miser?

Just then there was a rustle of wings, a quick flap-flapping. A crow appeared on the windowsill. It was a giant black crow. It cawed loudly. Fern knew she was being scolded. Was it the Miser, transformed? She quickly put the letters back in their envelopes and under the bed.

"Sorry," Fern said.

The crow looked at her sadly. It cawed again, a high cry. Fern thought the crow might hop to her and sit in her lap. It seemed so forlorn. But, no, the crow puffed up its chest. It began beating the air. It rushed at Fern, and she screamed. She ran out the bedroom door, and the crow was after her. She turned and ran down the stairs, past her black umbrella in the parlor, through the kitchen and out the back door to the yard. She felt the crow flap violently around her, up, up into the sky.

Fern stood there, breathing hard, with her hands on her hips. Had the Miser, in the shape of a crow, just caught her with his secret? Or had it been a crow? Sometimes a crow is just a crow.

Out in the distance, she saw a shape stand up in the garden. It looked like Mrs. Appleplum, her dress, her swoop of hair; but she was standing upright, not hunched even the least little bit. In fact, she seemed rather tall. She was striding confidently around the garden with a set of clippers. She stopped suddenly as if she felt Fern watching her. She looked up, then rummaged through her pocket. She held up a letter over her head. Fern walked toward her, and she walked toward Fern. They met in the middle of the yard. There was nothing arthritic about Mrs. Appleplum now. Nothing at all, except for a small limp, just a little limp in one leg. It reminded Fern of the bird that turned into a dog. Fern's

heart was pounding in her chest.

"This is for you," her grandmother said. She handed the letter to Fern, and Fern recognized the handwriting—the Miser's.

Fern took the letter, but her head was spinning. Shaken by the angry crow in the Miser's room and by having just been at her old house, which was not her home—it had never really been her home—Fern wanted to confess to Mrs. Appleplum, more than ever before, that she was not Ida Bibb, but her granddaughter. She remembered the kiss Mrs. Appleplum had given her on her cheek and how she had wanted to hug her after dealing with all of the creatures in the yard. Fern remembered how it had felt to have her hand in the goldfish pond that first time. She said, "I . . . I . . . haven't been honest."

"It's okay," the old woman said. "I haven't been honest either."

"Your name is Dorathea Gretel. I know, but . . ."

"Yes, and you know I have a limp from an accident. You know about the accident too, don't you? You saw me once get hit by a car, but you didn't know it was me. I thought you might put it together though. So I took on many limps so that you wouldn't recognize that limp. You're very smart, *Fern*."

Fern looked at her. Her eyes welled up. Her heart swelled. Her grandmother knew who she was, had always known. Had she known her since she was just a baby? "When I was a little," Fern said, "there was a book, and I shook crickets out of it, a whole roomful!" It felt wonderful to be able to tell her anything she wanted, anything at all.

Mrs. Appleplum smiled and shook her head. "Things aren't always what they seem, are they?"

Fern remembered the snowflakes that had turned into scraps of paper and the little sentence—*that* little sentence, that she had lined up on her desk. "No," she said. "They aren't."

Mrs. Appleplum pulled Fern to her chest. She hugged her tightly. She smelled of sweet lemons and the garden's dirt. And Fern knew that Mrs. Appleplum had been keeping an eye on her for a long time. She'd been the bird on her windowsill, and the bat that had turned into the marble. She'd been the tree and the nun and the lamppost, and she'd known everything all along.

"Do you want your umbrella back?" Fern asked.

"That old thing? No, thank you. I'm not sure why you held on to it. It's dented, you know."

This made Fern laugh and cry at the same time. Has that ever happened to you? It's such a strange and wonderful thing. If it hasn't ever happened to you, I hope it does one day.

"Hush, my girl, hush. We've got work to do," Fern's grandmother said. "The Bone is gone."

PART 5

SWEET, SWEET

THE KIDNAPPING
(actually, The Adultnapping, right?)

FERN TORE TO THE FRONT YARD, WHERE SHE found the Bone's old jalopy, its hood still cranked open. Her grandmother called her to the house. Fern ran to her, ripped open the letter her grandmother had been holding and read it out loud while following her grandmother upstairs.

Dear Fern,

I have the Bone. I want the book. I believe you've heard of <u>The Art of Being Anybody</u>? I'll come to collect it at three o'clock. Don't try to find us. We'll find you. If I don't have it today. I'll have to do something terrible to the Bone. I don't want to do this terrible thing. But as you know, I haven't been myself.

Sincerely,

M.

Fern began, "Do you know—"

"The Miser, yes. He was a fine enough boy. His name was Michael, once upon a time. Your mother cared for him, but didn't love him."

"Did you know—"

"I knew Mr. Haiserblaitherness was the Miser, certainly. Just as I knew you and your father were never the Bibbs."

"And Mr. and Mrs. Drudger . . ."

"They are nice people, Fern. They took care of you well. A bit dull, but nice."

"How come—"

"You could get crickets to pop out of a book as a little, little girl, but now you have to relearn it? Well, children can do so many things until they're told they can't. This is true of you, as an Anybody, but it's true for other children, too."

"You've been . . ."

Here Fern's grandmother turned. They now stood near the entranceway to her grandmother's bedroom.

It was the only room in the house Fern hadn't seen yet. "Yes, I've been the one keeping an eye on you. I knew that you would come to me, when you needed me. In your own time. This is the way it was meant to work, Fern."

"Do you know—"

"Of course I know where *The Art of Being Anybody* is. Do you think I'd leave it laying about?"

Her grandmother twisted the knob and opened the door. Inside was a jungle of books, and everything in it, truly everything, was made of books—the night stand, the dresser, even the bookcase that held books was made of books. The bed had a coverlet, dust ruffle, and canopy of soft, old canvaslike parchment with ancient scrawl. The curtains were made of the same material. The lamp shade was an octagon of thin books wired together. Fern turned and turned in the room, the ceiling, the walls—all books. The floor, too, was completely covered by leather bindings, like a brick path. She bent down and opened the book at her feet: *Admiral Hornblower in the West Indies*. She went to pick it up off the floor.

"I wouldn't do that, if I were you. Those books aren't lying on the floor. They *are* the floor. If you lie on your belly, though, you can still read it."

"Maybe later," Fern said.

Her grandmother smiled. "When I give you *The Art of Being Anybody*, Fern," she said, "you can do anything with it. I mean anything. You can use it in such a way that, eventually, one day, you could be a world leader. In fact, if you learn everything it has to offer, you could rule the world. Do you understand?"

"I don't want to rule the world. I want the Bone back."

Her grandmother shook her head. "I've heard this before, you know. It's what your mother said when the Bone was coming for her. We were standing in this very room. And do you know what I said?"

"No," Fern said.

"I told her that she could take the book, but that she was making a mistake by going off with the Bone. A terrible mistake."

"But, but—"

"I know now," Fern's grandmother said. "I know now that she was right. The Bone found the ladder behind the barn, and when he got to the top of it, Eliza was there—her face flushed and bright. She chose love or it chose her. Love, Fern. And when she called me from the hospital, she told me that lying beside her was the book. She told me that I should come and get it, later, after. 'After what?' I asked. But she didn't answer. I went to the hospital. And she was gone. I told this anxious, sputtering nurse that I wanted to look at the babies. She took me to a window, and I looked out over the sea of faces. I found you, and I knew you were one of ours. 'There,' the nurse said. 'There he is. Baby Boy Bone.' And she was pointing to a squinty baby in a blue blanket. I knew she was wrong, but I didn't say a word. Fate. I knew it was fate. I shouldn't interfere, that you would come to me, one day. I cried and cried. I said, 'I'll see you again, Baby Girl Drudger.' And I took the book."

Fern was crying now, tears streaming down her face. Her grandmother lifted her chin with her hand. "Do you know why the Bone is called the Bone?"

Fern shook her head. She'd asked once but the question had ruffled the Bone, and so she never pursued it.

"Eliza told me his mother named him that when he was a baby because he was so sweet that it seemed he had an extra bone in his body, a sweet bone."

"He thinks he's tough," Fern said, smiling.

Mrs. Appleplum smiled. "Let's go save him." She opened a drawer on her bedside table—the one spot where you'd expect someone to put a book, the most obvious spot—and she pulled out a big leather-bound book with a thin leather belt around it, just as the Bone had described. It had gold lettering on its front cover: THE ART OF BEING ANYBODY; under it, in smaller gold letters: OGLETHORP HENCEFORTHTOWITH.

"Here," said Mrs. Appleplum, "open it." She handed Fern the book, and Fern took its heavy weight into her arms. She closed her eyes, held the book to her chest and thought of how her mother once had held this exact same book the exact same way. She ran her hand over the gold letters and along the thin leather belt. "Go on," Mrs. Appleplum urged.

Fern unhooked the belt and opened the book, but just as the Bone had warned her, it made no sense. It was in an awful, jumbled mess. Unlike Fern's mother's diary, there would be an occasional word, a terrible, senseless word like "notwithstanding" or "aforementioned," but that was it. "I can't read it," Fern admitted.

Mrs. Appleplum took the book back. First she pulled a purple crayon from her pocket. "No, no, not this one," she said. Next she found a black ink pen. "Of course you can't read this book. You can't read it any more than I can. This book doesn't belong to you!" Her grandmother showed her the first page of the book, where there was a sign you see in many books. It read, THIS BOOK BELONGS TO: and there was a list of names. The last on the list was Eliza, just that—Eliza. Fern's grandmother said, "Do you know why your mother was such a good Anybody?"

Fern shook her head.

"She knew who she was, deep down. To become someone else or something else you have to know yourself first." She handed her the pen. "Write your name," she said.

Fern thought a moment. Who was she? She wasn't

Fern Drudger. She wasn't ever really. She wasn't Ida Bibb. She hadn't ever been called Fern Bone and she hadn't ever been called Fern Gretel, her grandmother's last name. She could say that she was the Bone's daughter or she could say she was Mrs. Appleplum's granddaughter. But none of those things seemed to fit. And so she simply wrote FERN, in small letters, and that seemed right.

"Now close the book and open it again."

Fern did just that, and when she opened it to a page in the middle of the book, every word was clear. In fact, the page she turned to was Chapter Six: Hypnotizing and Dehypnotizing Objects. Fern thought of her mother's diary. Maybe it wasn't in code after all, but hypnotized! "When trying to dehypnotize said book, it is best and most appropriate to concentrate, ruminate and cogitate on the binding first, just as it's best to concentrate on a beak when transforming into a bird. . . ."

"Now the book is yours," her grandmother said. "Oglethorp Henceforthtowith had the ability to hypnotize objects, such as books, as well as people. So he wrote this book and then hypnotized it so that it could only be read by its owner. Wasn't he a very smart writer?" The Henceforthtowiths have a long and sordid history—some wondrous and some dastardly. I won't go into it in this book. It would be too overwhelming, for you and for me. But the answer to this question was yes,

Oglethorp Henceforthtowith was a very, very smart writer. Very smart. Very smart indeed.

Fern closed the book, rehooking its belt. She had one more question, though. There was one thing she thought she needed to put into action before going to save the Bone. She wasn't sure why she felt she had to do it, but she was sure it was important, urgent. She said, "I think it's better to tell people how you feel and not keep it bottled up, don't you?"

"Yes, I do," her grandmother said.

"Well, then, there's some mail that needs to be delivered. And I think I'll need an army to do it."

ARMED WITH A BOOK

IF YOU WERE GOING TO TAKE ON SOMEONE LIKE the Miser in, let's say, an old abandoned gas station where your father was being held captive, and you could shake a book and make something from inside that book pop out of it—and perhaps you can, what do I know?—what book would you choose?

The Bible? Did someone say the Bible? Yes, yes, smart thinking. But what if the Red Sea pours out? Do you even know how to part the Red Sea? No, I didn't think so.

Did someone say King Arthur? Well, that's a fine guess. Except of course the horses could get all tangled up on the way out, which is cruelty to animals and therefore illegal. And what if all of those knights don't know whom they're supposed to conquer, and they turn on you?

Did someone say Robin Hood? I heard someone say Robin Hood, very softly, someone being almost too shy to say anything at all. Robin Hood is always a nice choice if you're looking for a hero. But quite frankly the whole damsel-in-distress bit turns me off. Robin Hood goes around thinking that women can't take care of themselves, and women can, for goodness sake, especially in this day and age! Especially Fern!

Fern wanted to bring her mother's diary. That was a thought that crossed her mind, but it was with Howard, although now she knew Howard wouldn't really be able to decode it since it was most likely not in code, but hypnotized. Fern thought for a minute about what other book she could bring instead—one that could save her and the Bone. It didn't take her long to figure out. She wanted to save the Bone herself. That meant there was only one sensible book to bring along—her own diary. This is important to remember. Sometimes you need to dig down deep, to rely on your own resources. This is a very American thing, self-reliance. Our forefathers and our foremothers, and, for that matter, our foreaunts and foreuncles, would say that self-reliance is a cornerstone of something or other.

I've lost my train of thought, but hopefully you know what I mean. Self-reliance. Fern trusted herself—now that she knew who she was—and she brought her own diary because she knew that she could trust it. In short, she had faith in herself.

Fern held her diary close to her heart. She had *The Art of Being Anybody* in her lap as she and her grandmother were bumping along back roads in her grandmother's truck.

"It's an old gas station," Fern told her. "The pumps look ancient. It's abandoned. It seems like a perfect spot."

"Yes, yes," her grandmother said. "I know the one. I know! How smart of you."

"I come by it naturally, Dorathea Gretel!" Fern said, trying out the name for the first time. "Dorathea Gretel. Dorathea Gretel . . ." There was something about it she liked very much.

The road was dusty and pocked with potholes. "Are we almost there?"

"Almost."

Meanwhile, the army of fairies had Mrs. Appleplum's address stamp and an ink pad. They were stamping Mrs. Appleplum's address on each letter as the return address. The mailman would be there soon and so they were working fast, buzzing like a hive, the droning hum of wings. Above the dull roar, the red-headed fairy was barking orders. "Go, go, go!" she shouted. "We've got orders to follow!"

Meanwhile, Howard was feeding Mr. and Mrs. Drudger monkey food that he'd ordered through the Internet. He'd been to the bank with Mr. Drudger dressed as an ape, and things had gone well. Mr. Drudger was a hit. A mother with two young kids asked Howard if his father did birthday parties. Howard said yes and gave the woman their phone number. The Drudgers seemed to enjoy the monkey chow, and it was quiet enough for the moment so that Howard could pore over Eliza Bone's diary. He saw no patterns emerging. Nothing, which isn't really a surprise to us, now, is it?

And the Bone? Well, Fern was right. He was in the garage of an old gas station, one that he remembered from his youth. They used to spend long afternoons there together—Eliza, the Bone, and the Miser—listening to old records. The Bone remembered it all—the oil stains, the dust, the stacked antiques, the smell of grease. But now the Bone was tied to a chair. He was concentrating on the Great Realdo. He was thinking, *I need you. Where are you?* The Miser was pacing in front of him, pacing, pacing. His spies were gathered by the front door, keeping guard.

"You are a thief, Bone. You stole Eliza from me."

"No, she chose me. There was nothing I could do. I loved her," the Bone said.

"No, you were a sneak. You hypnotized her into loving you. And I wasn't powerful enough to turn her love back to me. But who's more powerful now? I am! And I will have my way!"

"But remember when we were kids, riding unicycles together? We were best friends. Remember you used to be—" the Bone said.

"Shut up!" the Miser yelled.

"You used to be—"

"Stop it!"

"You used to be so sweet, so kindhearted!"

"I have not been myself! And it's your fault, Bone. Your fault! If you were dead, maybe then everything would be better!"

Fern and her grandmother parked right in front of the old station. The red van with its gold lettering—HAISERBLAITHERNESS LIGHTS, PLASTICS, AND TOILETRIES—was parked near the pumps, as if gassing up. "You go in, Fern," her grandmother said. "You can do it."

"By myself?"

"Yes!" her grandmother urged.

"But he's not alone!"

"You'll do wonderfully."

"No, I can't. I need help."

"You have all the help you need." Her grandmother nodded at the books in Fern's arms.

Fern popped open the door and slid off the seat to her feet. "Wish me luck."

"You don't need luck," her grandmother told her.

Fern closed the car door and walked toward the gas station, the books clamped to her chest.

THE DUEL 3

FERN KNOCKED ON THE DOOR. THERE WERE LOUD rummaging sounds and lots of whispery voices. "It's her," she heard. "She's here." The door opened slowly, but the entrance was blocked by a row of small, tightly muscled bodies—the Miser's spies. They wore matching red jumpsuits that had HAISERBLAITHERNESS LIGHTS, PLASTICS, AND TOILETRIES stitched in gold letters over small pockets on their chests. Some stood with their arms crossed and eyed Fern menacingly, while others seemed edgy, nearly frantic, glancing around excitedly.

"What do you want?" one asked in a loud voice; then he added in a whisper, "You should go. He's in no mood."

"I want to see the Miser," Fern told them, jutting out her jaw proudly.

"You aren't supposed to be here," one from the back said urgently. "You should go, go on home!"

"Is something wrong?" Fern asked.

"No, no," they all said too quickly, some wagging their heads no, others nodding.

"She's here!" a spy called out. "She's right here! Now! At the door."

Fern heard the Miser growl. "Not now!" he said.

"Yes!" another spy piped up. "Right now!"

"Get going!" the Miser's voice boomed from inside the garage. "I don't need any of you!"

And so the spies ran off. One muttered, "Best of luck." They raced to the red van, each jumping up the step. The engine revved quickly, and the van sped off in a whirl of dust.

Something was wrong. Fern knew it. She was certain of it. The Miser had been thrown off his plan somehow. Fern stepped deeper into the garage. He looked worn down, furious, but with a weariness in his eyes.

"Do you have the book?" the Miser asked, sneering at Fern. He was trembling with nerves.

"I do, but I want to see the Bone first. I want to make sure he's safe."

"Don't make me angry!" the Miser said, but it wasn't so much threatening as it was pleading.

"I want to see him now!" Fern said, and she tried to push her way past the Miser, but he was too strong. Fern could feel her grandmother watching her from the car. Her grandmother had faith in her. Fern had faith in herself. She dropped to the ground quickly and dashed between the Miser's legs.

"Bone?" she cried, racing around the garage. "Bone? Where are you?"

But the Bone was gone. All that sat there was an old wooden chair with ropes tied loosely around it. There was no back door. Fern wondered where the Bone could have gone. How had he escaped? She felt a rise of chatter inside herself. She would have to start her talking. She could feel it. But then she held the books tighter to her chest. *There's no time for that,* Fern thought to herself. *I don't need to chatter. I need to think clearly and calmly, to be strong.*

She was right. There was no time. She heard a high-pitched howl, a screech. There was a breeze, then another breeze, then another breeze. She turned around slowly, ever so slowly. The flapping of enormous wings, a long neck, and a pointy snapping beak. The Miser had become a vulture.

This was worse than Fern had expected. She opened her diary. While holding on tight to *The Art of Being Anybody*, she shook the diary as best she could, hoping something good would slip out—something to help her. She shook and she shook. The Miser was flapping harder now. The room was gusty. Some loose pages of sheet music in the corner rose up and swirled. The vulture screeched again. The first thing to plop out was a plump, drowsy hobbit.

"What? Where?" he sputtered. The vulture swooped over his head and the hobbit scrambled under a table.

"Sorry!" Fern said.

She shook some more and books tumbled out, a small pile. A book spilling books, not surprising at this point. She shook again, and there was Mary Curtain, the flustered nurse who'd accidentally swapped Howard and Fern so many years ago, sprawled on the floor in a flowered house dress and apron. Fern recognized her because, well, Marty had done a good job of being Mary Curtain after all. He'd looked just like her, and Fern had written about the real Mary Curtain in her diary, a good bit, in fact.

"Excuse me!" she said. "I don't know how . . . I was cooking muffins!" In fact, she was still wearing her oven mitts. "My husband will wonder . . . He's watching his favorite TV program and—"

But she had no time to finish the sentence. Fern was still shaking when out swung a bowling ball, connected to an arm, and Marty came flying out behind it, right into Mary Curtain, bowling her over.

"Who are you?" Mary Curtain asked.

"I was about to bowl on lane eight! I'm . . . Hey, you're Mary Curtain, the nurse," Marty said.

"Marty? Is that you?"

But there was no time for further hellos. The vulture let out a sharp cry, and Mary did too.

"What's this?" Marty asked, tucking his bowling ball under his arm.

"Don't ask," Fern said, shaking the book some more. "Just get under there." She pointed to the hobbit, who smiled awkwardly, trying to make the best of the situation. The vulture squawked again, and Mary and Marty did as they were told.

"C'mon!" Fern urged, rattling the diary with all her might. "C'mon now!" But Fern's diary had almost no weight to it. She felt a rise of panic. What if it was refusing to give anything else? It felt empty.

And then, miraculously, there was a glimpse of blue. A butterfly flapped from the pages. A butterfly? How was that supposed to help her? But, no, she'd written about the Great Realdo. She'd written about the Bone being visited by the butterfly while getting the ladder to climb to Eliza's room that night so many years ago. Had the Great Realdo come to help her?

The butterfly climbed and darted through the air. It flapped clumsily toward the vulture. Fern wanted to make a break for the door, but still couldn't. There was only one door, and all of the action was taking place in front of it. She squatted down under an old wooden desk across from Mary, Marty, and the hobbit. She was still clutching the two books. The vulture beat at the butterfly with its tough wings, lunging and snapping. But the butterfly just skittered along, bouncing around in front of the vulture's face.

This only made the Miser angrier. He grew big furry clawed feet. The wings shrank and his teeth grew. His head became blunt, golden, and then sprouted a wild mane . . . a lion.

"Oh, my!" Mary Curtain squealed, grabbing on to the hobbit, who was wide-eyed and confused.

Just then the butterfly dipped to the ground. It began to shake its wings, and soon it had trembled into a tiny, speedy mouse.

"The Great Realdo. . . ," Fern whispered in awe.

The brown field mouse tore around, zigzagging under the lion's paws. The lion's mouth lathered. It pounced this way and that, but always too late. The big beast grew mad and dizzy, finally breathless.

Fern crawled to the back of the garage. She rubbed circles on the back windows. She was looking for the Bone. She didn't see him. She glanced around the garage again. The lion was staggering away from the front door. Now she might be able to get out. In fact, Mary Curtain had grabbed the hobbit and was running for the door with him clutched to her bosom like a baby. Marty was close behind, still holding tight to his bowling ball. The Great Realdo, as a little mouse, was squeaking at Fern, and seemed to be saying *Go, go now*.

Fern was thinking back. She was trying to remember that first car ride in the old jalopy with Marty disguised as Mary Curtain. What had the Bone said when she asked him about transforming into a bird then a dog? *Maybe, just maybe, if our lives depended on it, we could have some great sparkling moment. . . .* What if the Bone didn't get away? What if he was still right here? What if he transformed into the chair? The ropes?

But this musing didn't last long. The Miser was convulsing. His body was rattling into some new shape. He was growing leathery, scaled. His shoulders broadened. He stood hunched on two large clawed feet, his forearms shrank, hung as two claws at his chest. Muscled, vicious, hulking. The Miser was now a dinosaur. Fern didn't have perfect knowledge of dinosaurs. An oviraptor? She knew some random facts about meat eaters, *T. rex*. She'd read about paleontologists. She stood in the dinosaur's looming shadow. He was no longer distracted by the mouse. He walked toward her, roaring now, his thick nails clicking. He clawed the air.

The mouse was darting around nervously. The Great Realdo didn't seem to know what to do. Fern thought as hard as she could. What had she read about oviraptors? Something, something about the males . . . they protected their eggs! That was it. Once they were thought to steal eggs, but someone had discovered that they weren't thieves, they were proud fathers.

"Egg!" Fern yelled to the mouse. "Become an oviraptor's egg!"

The mouse scurried to a spot on the ground between Fern and the dinosaur. It trembled and then bloated to the size and shape of a huge speckled egg. The Miser, despite himself, turned his gaze on the egg. He snatched it up in his front claws and took it to the far end of the

room, where he curled around it lovingly. In moments, he was fast asleep.

Fern jumped up and began shuffling through the stacks of old things—warped golf shoes, rusted flour sifters and sugar canisters—as fast as she could. "Bone?" she said. "Bone?"

Fern felt frantic. She accidentally knocked over an old trombone, which hit a stack of slippery records. One jostled the record player, flipping a switch. The old thing hummed. Its arm popped up and the needle moved over to the record. It all happened so fast that Fern couldn't get to it in time. The record started up: "Sweet, sweet, my sweet darling angel, where have you gone, where have you gone?"

But it wasn't anyone famous singing—it wasn't Elvis or a Beatle or anything—it was the Bone's voice. Fern would recognize it anywhere.

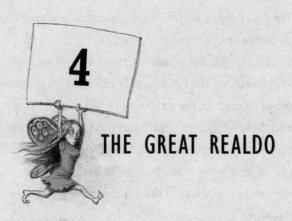

4

THE GREAT REALDO

ANNE OF GREEN GABLES NEVER HAD TO DEAL
with such a mess. Neither did Heidi with her grandpa
in Norway or wherever.

Fern's father was a record spinning on an old
turntable in an old gas station. Her father's greatest
enemy was a dinosaur asleep on the floor a few feet
away. Her father's greatest hero of all time was a big
speckled egg in the dinosaur's clutch. She was worried
about an army of fairies and if they had succeeded in
mailing an enormous collection of letters. And the
people she'd always thought were her parents, Mr.
and Mrs. Drudger, were locked up in their house
where they were under the impression that they were

monkeys. And Howard, her swapped brother of sorts, was trying to decode her mother's diary, in vain. Fern's mother had been a very talented Anybody. Fern's mother was still dead.

Fern needed help. *Luckily,* Fern thought, *my grandmother is in her truck right out front.*

She ran to the parking area in front of the old gas station, still clutching the book and her diary. Her grandmother wasn't there. In the cab of the truck sat the stray hobbit and Mary Curtain and Marty. Mary rolled the window down a few inches. "Is it safe?"

"I was bowling a good game, too!" Marty pouted. "I had three strikes already. Did I mention it was the championships?"

"Stay here," Fern said.

Her grandmother was missing. This didn't surprise Fern, not really. She knew that she had to figure this out on her own.

Fern walked back into the garage. The Miser was still asleep, but his dinosaur teeth were shrinking, his claws were plumping into pink fingers. Slowly, slowly, he was turning back into the Miser. The egg was snug tight to his belly. The record was still turning, the Bone's sweet, warbly voice crooning away about lost love.

Now, how would Fern get the Bone to be the Bone again? She thought again of Marty in the old jalopy, talking about how the Bone once became a four-legged, furry almost-dog. Marty had said he was lucky he didn't get stuck that way. It took all the concentration Eliza and Marty had to get him back. And the Bone had mentioned that third ingredient, the one he'd lost. But wasn't he getting better and better? Wasn't he improving now that Fern was helping him? He'd mastered not only Mr. Bibb's nose, but also the mustache and an occasionally genuine admiration for encyclopedias. She listened to the song, the "sweet, sweet," the "my darling angel, where have you gone?" She thought of the Bone and his misty eyes and how much he'd loved Fern's mother, and her love for him must have seemed like it had disappeared when she died.

Could the ingredient be love? Fern loved the Bone. She truly did.

She placed both hands on the record player. She thought about the Bone—soft, sweet, with gentle eyes. She closed her eyes and thought about how much she loved him. He was her father, her wonderful, sweet father. She knew this absolutely, deep in her heart. She felt an electrical energy, a revving motor, like an engine catching and purring to life. The record player lost its hard edges. It grew warm. Fern watched it quake and twist, blushing with the green of the Bone's shirt. And then his face bloomed, a popping open of arms and legs. The Bone.

He grabbed Fern and hugged her. "Fern! I knew you'd find me! I knew you would!" He pulled away and looked at her, just taking her in. "Fern, my girl." And he hugged her again. Fern wrapped her arms around him too. It was the first time they'd hugged each other, and the Bone started crying. It was like something in him broke and tears came streaming down his face. "I love you, Fern! My darling daughter! I love you!"

"I love you, too," she said, and she knew it was true because love was the ingredient that had brought him back. They hugged and hugged until the Bone looked around, as if realizing where he was for the first time. "The Great Realdo came as a butterfly at first," Fern explained. "Just like you told me he would."

"Where is he?"

Fern took the Bone by the hand and showed him the Miser. His skin was still leather, his snout long and tough. "There," Fern said, pointing to the egg. "That's the Great Realdo. It's really him!"

Just then the egg rolled out of the Miser's hands. It wobbled toward Fern and the Bone, then stopped. It quivered twice, and then its shell started to crack as if there were a tiny baby dinosaur inside, pushing to get out. But there was no sharp egg tooth. No, there was a nose, two big wet-looking eyes, and then an orthopedic shoe. And *pop!* In one enormous heap—Mrs. Appleplum. Dorathea Gretel. Fern's grandmother.

"You? Is it you?" Fern asked.

"You can't be the Great Realdo!" the Bone said.

"Yes," Fern said. "Yes, she can!" Fern remembered the story that the Bone had told her—the butterfly sitting on his shoulder as Eliza appeared at her bedroom window that night years ago. And her grandmother had told her that, too. She'd said, "Eliza was soon there—her face flushed and bright." And something had seemed off to Fern when she heard her grandmother say that. It was like her grandmother had seen her daughter, too, in the window— and she had! She had! She'd been sitting on the Bone's shoulder all along. She didn't want her daughter to go, but she knew she'd chosen love. The Bone needed to find the ladder, and so Fern's grandmother made sure he did.

There was something else, too. "Dorathea Gretel. It's a strange name," Fern said. She looked at the Bone. "Don't you think?" The Bone stared at her blankly. Fern was thinking back to the little slips of paper she'd arranged and rearranged as a child on her desk, the slips of paper that had started out as snow. "If you switch the letters around. . . ," Fern said.

"The Great Realdo!" said the Bone.

Fern's grandmother winked one beautiful, big eye.

Fern and the Bone couldn't help it: they both winked back.

THE END OR JUST THE BEGINNING

I'VE HEARD STORYTELLERS SAY THAT SOMETIMES they feel like magicians. They can make things appear and disappear with poofs and smoke, and have some old guy playing the organ to make things seem spookier. But I don't feel like a magician. I feel more like a rabbit nervously pooping in the magician's tight satin top hat or, worse, a rumple-winged dove shoved up some narrow sleeve. I'm hoping someone will pull me out of this tale so my ears can flop open or so my feathers can flap back into place, and then I can see what's really going on around me, blinking into some spotlight. (My dear old writing teacher would never have admitted to such fears, but, let's be honest, despite all of his big awards and his "begin at the beginning" and his "be true to the story," he's a big drafty windbag, and I've got to forge on alone, as we all must do at some point in our lives.)

You see, I think I know you pretty well. You're right on top of everything, every little detail. And you want to know this: if the missing ingredient was love, then how was it that the Miser, so loveless, became such an expert Anybody?

I can only give my theory, and here's a tip: When grown-ups say they've got a theory, it means they really don't know and are about to make something up to suit themselves. So here goes—the letters. The Miser had to write the letters because he really was, deep down, from the day he was born into this world, a good person. But rejection and loss, these are difficult to bear, and I hope you don't learn that the hard way. I suppose, though, that the hard way may be the only way to really learn it. I mean, you can watch after-school specials dealing with tough topics, but they don't ever really cut the mustard.

When Eliza ran off with the Bone, the Miser lost his love and his best friend. Instead of getting over it, he let it consume him, turn him into a different kind of person altogether. (Remember how he signed all his letters? Of course you do.) He still had love, but he couldn't show it anymore. Now I'm no psychologist who's going to sort through the Miser's mental closet and try to rehang his pants so the pleats stay creased, but maybe he was afraid of more rejection. So he wrote the letters but couldn't send them. He was hoarding love, in a way. He was storing it up by not giving it to anyone. Like those people who stack their basements with canned corn, bottled water, and flashlights, thinking the end of the world is coming, the Miser had built up a surplus, a little arsenal of love.

Now, the Miser was finally back in his room in bed, and weak from all of that transforming. Mary Curtain was also at the house. She called her husband, Emil, and told him to take the muffins out of the oven. He said he didn't know how to work an oven. She said, "Well, I'm needed here, Emil. I'm a nurse, you know, and someone is ill. You'll just have to learn how to work the oven."

And she became an efficient steam engine of energy. She took the Miser's temperature. She applied cool compresses. She made him some tea and toast. The house of books was surprising to her, but she moved through it efficiently. It was a long time since she'd been a nurse, but it felt good to be a true woman of science again, one with a mission.

While Nurse Curtain was downstairs concocting her remedies (and Marty was back for the last round of his bowling tournament, which they won because of the rallying power of his team who, in the big game, with a man down and under pressure, stepped up their game, despite the odds—a heartwarming story of bowling and determination), Fern thought this might be a good time to break it to the Miser that the letters had been mailed—they had, you know. The fairies had done very good work and Fern had shaken them all back into their book, where they remain quite happy, according to my research.

Fern and the Bone went to the Miser's room. He was lying in bed, completely limp. Every once in a while his eyes would open. It was the first time Fern had ever really seen his eyes. They'd always been covered up by Mr. Haiserblaitherness's eyebrows. They were pretty green eyes with soft black lashes.

"Miser," Fern said softly. "Michael?"

He looked up at her and nodded.

"I have something to tell you," Fern said. "We

mailed all of your letters."

"They were all stamped and ready to go," the Bone added. "We figured you meant to send them on . . . right?"

The Miser moaned. "No," he said. "No, no." He tried to reach out to the Bone, as if to strangle him, but he didn't have the strength. He flopped back onto his bed. He stared at the ceiling. "Hmm," he said. "I'm feeling . . ."

"What?" Fern asked.

"Well, that might explain why I'm feeling . . ."

"What is it?" the Bone said.

"I'm feeling more like myself," he said. And then he sighed, smiled and fell back to sleep.

The letters were bouncing around in a sack in the back of a mail jeep that had crisscrossed its route and was now on its way back to the post office. The letters would soon fly off in different directions. They would be popped into mailboxes and dropped through mail slots. In the weeks to come, visitors would show up at Dorathea's door, one after the other, to see the Miser, although some would call him Michael and others Chatbox, a childhood nickname. The spies showed up, one here and one there, weepy, clutching sweet, elegant letters filled with thanks and kindness. His sister Imogene would come and the grocer, now her husband.

When the Miser's mother would arrive, Nurse Curtain would hand him over to her. Nurse Curtain would make sure that the hobbits were all very healthy and drinking only in moderation, and she would be ready to go home again where she would teach Emil the workings of the house and start to apply for some nursing jobs. The Miser's mother would tend to the Miser with tea and mineral salts. She would scold him for not sending the letters earlier, but, too, she would shower him with hugs and kisses. She would call him Snook'ems. His father was a great help around the house, because he was so ridiculously strong. He still would eat a nail or two, but only for reasons of nostalgia, not for show. All the while, letters for the Miser poured in, hundreds of them. Flowers. Telegrams. His letters had been beautiful and loving, after all, and they inspired people. The Miser took all of the affection in. He let it fatten his heart with love till it was a plump muscle pounding happily in his chest.

But would he ever forgive the Bone for stealing Eliza's heart? This is hard to say. His letters to the Bone arrived at Fern's grandmother's house. Like on many of the other envelopes, somebody had written "return to sender." They must have figured the Bone was gone for good. Maybe it was the neighbor lady who didn't like the rooster man or one of the clog-dancing Bartons. In any case, the letters showed up, and the Bone read them. Here is an example:

Dear Bone,

Today is the kind of summer day when the three of us used to laze around sipping sodas, trying to turn into bullfrogs. I miss those days, Bone. I can't help but think: How could you? You know how hard I take things. It's been years and still you make me boil. I feel like I could burst into flames. I never used to be so flammable. But as you know, I haven't been myself.

M.

The Bone would walk into a room. The Miser would turn away. Many times, the Bone would say, "Look, I'm sorry." But the Miser couldn't ever quite respond, not quite. His head would sag. He'd shake it woefully, but he couldn't say it was okay, over, old business, forgiven. And Fern felt sad about this, because, like her mother, she had failed to bring these two friends back together. She'd gotten close, so close. . . .

But I'm getting ahead of myself. None of this had happened yet. The Bone was in the kitchen, making dinner, while his mother-in-law read to him from a chair at the table. They'd made a deal. He and Fern were welcome to stay there as long as they wanted, but the Bone would take over the house, the yard, all the work and, in exchange, she would read to him— every darn classic she could get her hands on. And she could get her hands on a heck of a lot. Right now she was reading him a book about an Indian who lived in a cupboard, and it made the Bone open each of the cabinets very slowly and carefully, afraid an arrow might be slung in his direction. It was a different kind of house to read a book in.

Fern was up in the bedroom, alone. She was happy to be alone for the moment. She put her diary back in her bag but she held on to *The Art of Being Anybody*. She would need to visit Howard again soon to get her mother's diary back. Now that she knew it was hypnotized and not in code, she would have to take a different approach with it. She would have the summer, at least, but she knew it would come to an end. And would Howard and Fern be swapped back again? Would they return to their old lives for the school year, and then switch next summer and maybe on weekends now and then? Would it be okay to be back with the Drudgers? Wouldn't they be a little different after all of this too? Wouldn't they have to be, after spending the summer as monkeys? Fern could settle into her own room with its quiet lichen and her own library of books growing, growing up the walls. Her butterfly collection—it would have new meaning now that she'd seen her grandmother take shape as one. Everything would have new meaning. For example, she would know who the bird watching her on the limb outside her window was now, and she could invite that bird in. Or would Howard stay in her room? Would she stay here, with her grandmother reading to the Bone, the Miser recovering in his room, writing letters again hour after hour? Would Fern transplant her lichen, letting it grow on the slippery rocks by the pond in the painting of the goldfish and lily pads? Her lichen would like it there. And she could begin to study *The Art of Being Anybody* by Oglethorp Henceforthtowith.

This was too much to think about for very long, and it didn't really matter. Fern knew now that there was a place where she could be herself, where she fit in, where she could feel really and truly at home. She could go anywhere in the world, and these facts would remain true. So her thoughts moved on. . . .

There was something more immediate that Fern was still trying to figure out. Something. She knew her mother couldn't be shaken from the book. She knew her mother's body couldn't ever come back in any transformation. But what about a piece of her essence, her soul? When the Bone was the record player playing a record, it wasn't just his body, but some other part of him, too, that was sitting in that machine. Fern could hear it in his voice.

Fern put both of her hands on the book with its small leather belt, just as she had the record player; but this time she thought of her mother, swaying to the music on the record player, pregnant and dancing. She thought about how much she loved her. She concentrated with all of her might. And, yes, her hands grew warm and she felt a certain sweetness, a warm-chested ache of love, then an outpouring. And, miraculously, a flood of the scent of lilacs.

AFTERWORD

WELL, IT SEEMS THAT MY OLD WRITING TEACHER got his hands on this book somehow—anonymously, maybe even slipped under his front doormat in the middle of the night—and he wrote me a letter of response. I have enclosed a shortened version of his letter. I had to cut a good bit of it because it is longer than the book I wrote, but here is the shortened version:

Dear N. E. Bode:

Stop! Please do not continue writing this silly and idiotic nonsense.... [Here he went on for 63 pages categorizing what exactly he found silly and what exactly he found idiotic.]

Firstly, I don't enjoy being called a "dusty windbag."

Should I remind you of my many various literary awards? [Evidently the answer to this question was yes, because he went on for 78 pages detailing his wondrous career.]

Secondly, you are not a good writer, just as you were not a good student. In fact, you were the worst [here he used a word that I cannot repeat] *student I ever had. Always tardy, always shuffling around to sharpen a pencil or get a drink of water. Don't think I didn't notice you reading other authors' books hidden in your lap during class time. Your papers were always stained with jelly and, more than once, I had to wake you up in the middle of one of my most interesting speeches!* [Here he included the most interesting speeches that I may have slept through—— 329 pages.]

Thirdly, you say that this story is true, but <u>who</u> is going to believe <u>you</u>, N. E. Bode? I ask you again: Who will believe? <u>Who indeed!</u>

Sincerely,

I will not reveal the windbag's name. That would be disloyal. But you know that I know that he knows that we all know there is more to tell. In fact, as Fern starts to learn new talents by reading *The Art of Being Anybody*, she goes away to a summer camp especially for aspiring young Anybodies. There is a mystery that turns us back to the family of Oglethorp Henceforthtowith, author of *The Art of Being Anybody*, especially his grandson Bort!!! O. Henceforthtowith. (Bort!!! spells his name exactly as it is written here, with three exclamation marks, and it is pronounced loudly and with emotion. He isn't Bort. He's Bort!!!, if you follow me.) Oh, there is much to tell. And in the words of my famous writing teacher: Who will believe? *Who indeed!*

ACKNOWLEDGMENTS

SPECIAL THANKS TO: FRED CHAPPELL (WHO *IS* A magician and not a nervous magician's rabbit!), Alix Reid (who believes, indeed!), David G. W. Scott (you brilliant rascal!), Glenda (quite an outlandish character in her own right!), Bill (whose imagination is vast and astonishing!), grandmothers everywhere (especially my Southern belle!); and to my smart young readers: Anna Galati, Matthew Marshall, Shana Mattes, Molly, Cece, Phoebe, Finneas, and Theo.

Special thanks to Julianna Baggott, who gave me the go-ahead to go off. (If you're a grown-up, you should look for Julianna's books, which are, so far, these three novels: *Girl Talk*, *The Miss America Family*, and *The Madam*; as well as a book of poems: *This Country of Mothers*. If you aren't a grown-up, you should wait until you are and then go find them.)

And special thanks to *you*, yes, *you*! Are you really surprised? You shouldn't be—after all, I did dedicate the whole entire book to you. If it weren't for you, this book would be fairly useless, wouldn't it? I mean, it could prop up the uneven leg of a chair or something, but that would be a pretty sad destiny for a book! So, thank you. Really.